FOUNDATIONS

Copyright © 2021 Richard Holliday

All rights reserved. No part of this book may be reproduced or used in any manner without the prior written permission of the copyright owner, except for the use of brief quotations in a book review.

The right of Richard Holliday to be identified as the author of this work has been asserted by him in accordance with sections 77 and 78 of the Copyright, Designs and Patents Act 1988.

Paperback edition originally published October 2021. Edition 1.0

KDP (Paperback edition) ISBN 9798489070669

Cover design by GermanCreative

Author photograph by Mark Lever

Discover more of Richard Holliday's work at
richardholliday.co.uk

Happy 32nd Birthday Chris!

Thanks for your friendship and making TWN a reality! Not a word about typos!

All best,

31/10/2021

FOUNDATIONS

RICHARD HOLLIDAY

In an office where the phone never seemed to ring, when it did, it sent Deborah Wrenly flying.

'H-hello?' she answered, cradling the beige plastic handset in her dainty little hands. Quickly, she held the round earpiece to the side of her head with her shoulder. She hummed, then reached for a pencil. Her fingers sent it flying. She was trying to listen to the caller. She hummed monosyllabically. The pencil dropped to the floor with a wooden tring. 'Shit!'

'Sorry?' the voice on the line said. 'What was that?'

Deborah apologised, bending down to pick up the pencil. The chair scooched away from behind her. She grasped the pencil. As she did so, the door to the office from the street clattered open. She smiled, seeing the young man in a sleeveless jumper atop a shirt with a mop of dark brown hair move quickly inside, closing the door and arresting the gust of chilly autumn air that it had let in.

The young man, without even taking off his coat, cupped his hands and swooshed it behind Deborah, catching her off-guard with a whinny as his hand met her behind.

'Quit it, Steve!' she hissed to Norris, who smiled and took off his coat. She took the telephone handset and recovered pencil in the other, scrawling words dictated to her on the telephone. She hung up and swivelled, giving Stephen Norris a severe glower.

'Wasn't me, guv, honest,' he said.

'Like hell,' Deborah countered. 'Don't bother with that,' she said, noticing Norris was already getting papers from his desk. 'You can take this upstairs.' She waved the note at him. He took it.

'Who's this guy, Peterson? Can't he come here himself and deliver his bad news?'

'I've met him once. That was enough,' she said. 'Now go.'

Norris pulled himself up from his desk and signed theatrically, making for the back of the office and a small corridor that led to some stairs.

'Come in,' the voice on the other side of the door at the top of the stairs hummed. The knock on the door had to battle past rolls and rolls of drawings, plans and papers to reach the ears of Mr Herve Chivron, the proprietor and master of all he surveyed. Norris opened the door and stepped in. 'Ah, Norris, isn't it?'

'It is, yes, sir,' Norris said. Mr Chivron was always sir.

'I don't see any tea, so I suppose you've come to see me for another matter,' the older man said, wiping his brow. Chivron was fifteen years Norris' senior and wore those years as they came: wiry hair on a wiry-framed man who wore wiry spectacles that enlarged his eyeballs, the red veins tracing across the surface like rivers. Norris stepped forward and handed him the note. Chivron's face fell.

'Bad news?' Norris asked. '... sir?'

Chivron looked up, the note floating loose from his fingers to the desk. 'Cancel all my meetings. I've got to go on site and sort this mess he's made out,' he said, getting to his feet and flapping about finding his coat. 'We've been too complacent, letting him run everything.'

'Sir, we've not discussed the latest designs for the-'

'Yes, yes, it'll keep, we're in big trouble, Norris,' Chivron said. Then he paused. 'Bring your notes with you. You can see the site. Be a second pair of eyes. And arms, should Peterson be pissy.'

'Is he likely to be?' Norris asked.

'Unfortunately, more often than not. Even if this particular predicament is of his own creation. I bet it was Townsend.'

'Who's Townsend?'

'I'll explain. There's lots of little things you're not quite there with. Where are you parked? You did drive, didn't you?'

'Yes, yes, sir, I did,' Norris stammered.

'Good. You can drive me there.'

'Where is there?'

Chivron laughed only once. 'Where all our drawings are becoming reality. We hope, anyway. You ever been on site?'

'No,' Norris said. 'Only been here four months.'

Chivron let a slither of a smile cross his face. 'See the dream, then. See your drawings in concrete and steel. Let's go.'

Norris followed.

'Which one's yours, then?' Mr Chivron asked from the steps of the office.

'That one,' Norris said, puffing his chest out. In his pocket, his keys tinkled. He pulled them out and strode out across the street, unlocking the maroon-red Morris Marina. Pulling away, Norris noticed Mr Chivron reach into his pocket to pull out a cigarette. It rose to his lips. 'Sir,' Norris peeped. Mr Chivron ignored him. Norris kept watching, his eyes away from the road. The same hand reached in to the same pocket, pulling out a packet of matches.

HOOOOOONNNNKKKK

'Sir!' Norris yelped, then looked up. The big lorry in front of them veered away, and Norris grabbed the wheel. The Marina swerved back into its lane.

'Bloody hell, careful! Nearly had me as tomato soup on the front of that thing!'

'Sorry,' Norris chattered. 'But please, could you not?'

'Not what?'

Norris nodded. Mr Chivron brandished the cigarette. His eyes narrowed at Norris. 'This car was a birthday present from my parents. Twenty first. And to celebrate me getting the job. At the practise. In the office.'

'I see,' Mr Chivron said, settling into the seat. He poked the cigarette back into his pocket with the matches. 'I mean, it's all a bit traditional, isn't it?'

'You think so?'

'Where's the bravery in the design, Norris? I sincerely hope

British Leyland's design doesn't rub off on your work.'

'Oh, no, sir! We're doing so many exciting things.'

'Are we?' Mr Chivron said. He looked sideways at his young employee.

'Oh, yes. New houses, streets in the sky? What couldn't be more exciting than that?'

Mr Chivron smiled. 'Norris, I think you're right. It's just a shame, isn't it?' Norris didn't answer but instead drove. His silence spurred the older man on. 'I'll probably be dead before they recognise me for what I do. You know, they literally think Herve Chivron is a ten-a-penny designer of council estate drek. But we'll see, my boy. I'll build 'em better, cheaper, and fill the skies with wonder.'

Norris didn't say anything for a moment. 'Well, let's hope Peterson doesn't put a lid on this one.'

'Nothing could,' Mr Chivron said. 'Nothing can put a lid on my Tower but me. We get this right, Norris, and they won't be able to build them fast enough.'

Norris steered through the gate, the tyres crunching on loose gravel. The Marina pulled up in front of a wooden shack. This was the construction site office. Two doors clanked open and banged shut in quick succession.

Ahead, a man turned. Beyond the site was a sea of orange gravel against the grey, featureless sky that sucked the warmth out of anything it touched. Norris shivered.

'You've got some nerve,' Chivron said. The man in front didn't turn. 'Peterson!'

'Well, well, well,' the stocky man said, pivoting.

'Well, where is it?'

'Where's what?'

'The bloody Tower, you clown! We had strict deadlines. You should've been on the fourth floor by now. I just see a hole in the ground. You know the pressure we're under!'

Peterson shrugged. 'None of my fault, you see. Or the guys' fault, I'll add right now.'

'What guys?' Chivron asked. 'That one's pissing about shovelling sand and... well, where are the others?'

For a busy building site of the Borough's pride and joy, there was a distinct lack of activity. Norris wished he'd brought a camera to catch this for his dad - who always said council spent more time leaning against shovels than digging.

'We've made a discovery. Follow me.' Chivron did, with Norris close behind. 'Who's the pipsqueak?' Peterson said, without even turning.

'Norris, my new junior. Taken over where Latchley left off. Terrible business,' Chivron said to Peterson, who simply exchanged a knowing glance. 'Talented man, think he's got potential.'

'Hello,' Norris said, holding out a hand.

Peterson didn't react and carried on right past. He stopped at the foot of a large trench that criss-crossed the ground and formed the footings of the Tower to come. He said nothing. Peterson didn't even acknowledge Chivron's introduction of Norris.

'They're meant to be twelve feet deep. This is barely eight,' Chivron said. 'Have you been taking your eye off the ball, Peterson?'

'I don't much like your tone, Mr Chivron,' Peterson said, his voice forming a cloud that blotted the warmth from an already miserable day. 'I've had an associate on site every day that I've been... otherwise engaged. Now, let me show you the root of the problem and why we're not building high for happiness just yet.' Peterson indicated to a ladder down into the pit. 'I'll show you what we're up against. You first, pipsqueak,' Peterson said to Norris. Norris said nothing and descended into the pit. Chivron and Peterson followed, their feet stamping in muddy puddles, sending ripples flourishing across the dirty water.

'Sir,' Norris insisted again. 'What's the matter?'

'This should all be cement and concrete, Norris. He's been paid for it, but you don't know the shit I... we'll be in should we not be open in seventy-two. It'll take a monumental effort.'

'Come on, then,' Peterson called from the other side of the pit. Chivron and Norris followed to a deeper part of the excavation.

The architect arrived first. He glanced down. 'I see what you mean,' Chivron mumbled.

'What?' Norris called, finally arriving in a flourish of muddy splashes. He glanced down. 'Oh.'

Protruding from the entire corner of the excavation were stones... grey and regular shaped. Not stones, on closer inspection, but bricks. The outline of the bricks formed the corner of a rectangle. Contained in the rectangle were shards of calcified wood, frozen in time. Peters indicated behind. The two visitors turned, seeing rows of regularly spaced shadows erupting from the dirt. These weren't bricks, but stone tablets.

'They're grave markers,' Chivron realised. Norris turned back to the corner of bricks.

'And this, I bet, was the church.'

'This could be hundreds of years old. Maybe thousands.'

'Worse,' Peterson huffed, 'we can't get to the right depth to pour. It's all got to come up. Build the Tower on top of that lot and, well...' he started, making a creaking sound and gesturing with his arm, going from vertical to horizontal with an impression of a crash at the end.

'Then dig it up,' Chivron said. He reached into his pocket. He was going to have that damn cigarette now. Peterson did the same.

'Don't you think we've not tried?! Not that easy, Herve,' Peters breathed out. 'That stuff's like diamond. Something's holding it into the ground like glue. Oi, you!' He called to a workman above the pit, brandishing a pneumatic drill. 'Geddown here and give it a go. Show 'em.'

The navvy shook his head but made for the level. 'Didn' we go ov'r this before, Peterson, you git? And to bloody Townsend! Broke four bits and hardly chipped it.'

'Wasn't a survey done before you started digging?' Norris ventured. Peterson turned, took one look, and laughed, blowing smoke into the young man's face.

'Pipsqueak, you tell a good joke. Our survey meant diddly shit. Now we're wasted. Come on, Herve, let's talk turkey, eh? Hope you brought your chequebook.'

'Norris, hold the fort. This shouldn't take long.'

'Yes sir.'

Norris watched as Chivron and Peters hoisted themselves back up the ladder. He then turned, examining the stone on the very corner of the outline wall to the supposed chapel. Norris and touched it. The stone felt warm. Then he touched the adjacent stone, just a couple of inches next to it. It was cold.

'Fascinating,' the young man said to no-one. Behind him, Peters' workman huffed, ready to haul the pneumatic tool out of the pit.

'No, wait,' Norris said over his shoulder. He put his hand on the warm stone. It had already dried itself, while the others still were dark with dampness. It wobbled, a fissure opening underneath it. 'Can you stick that,' Norris said, referring to the drill, 'in there?'

The navvy squinted, then agreed. 'Get back and cover your ears. This thing makes quite a din, pip.'

Norris retreated, covering his ears. The workman pushed the loose stone forward with his boot. It pivoted in the ground like a loose tooth in an ancient set of gums. The tip of the pneumatic drill scraped into the abscess in the earth beneath. He then nodded, squeezing the twin triggers. The tip of the drill vibrated in a cloud of fine dust, the noise ratcheting past Norris' hands for a good few seconds.

Then the man withdrew. He pushed on the stone with his boot again. It wiggled, but no more than it had done before. 'Well that didn't do anythin',' the workman spat.

'Let me see,' Norris said, kneeling down. He touched the stone, but immediately he withdrew his hand with a hiss. It was boiling hot.

Then the ground creaked, solid earth groaning. From his knelt position, Norris felt it move. It dipped.

With a thud, the workman discarded the drill and scrambled up the ladder. 'Sod what you've done, pal,' he said. Norris turned back to watch, and at that moment the earth gave way beneath him. He screamed, but the scream stopped after just a moment, as he landed on something hard with a thud.

Norris opened his eyes. He was in darkness. Twelve feet above, a rough opening let in the sky. He got up. The ground felt solid. He reached forward but bumped into something about hip height.

'You alright down there, son?' the workman called.

'Yeah, yes,' Norris said. He took a big breath. The air felt... clear, the scent like that after summer rainfall. But it was a grisly autumn day. Through the opening above, the rain streamed in, seeming to evaporate as it crossed the threshold from the outside world into this strange space. 'Have you got a light?'

The workman disappeared from the opening but returned, throwing a torch to Norris, who switched it on.

'Whoa,' was all Norris could say as he swung the torch around. He stepped forward. What he was seeing couldn't be real. Stone walls surrounded the pit with elaborate carvings. The floor was smooth flagstone. And in the middle a rectangular object. Norris felt out and touched the wall. Cool stone, not slippery, but dry. As if it had been built yesterday.

Then he turned to the object in the centre. He took a step, then stopped.

'You okay down there, mate?' the workman called. Looking

up, Norris realised this wasn't just a pit, but something important. He waved the workman away, then turned back to the large object in the middle. He approached. It seemed to be festooned with twigs.

On closer inspection, the twigs were pearlescent. 'Bones,' Norris mouthed.

'Right, up you come!' the workman hollered from behind, hoisting a grubby ladder down. Norris went up, propelled by a strange draft that rattled the "twigs" atop the object.

Which Norris quickly recognised with a glance as a sarcophagus.

'The hell were you doing down there, pipsqueak?!' Peters bellowed from the top of the pit. 'Do you know how long this is going to take to fix, you stupid boy?!'

'But look,' Chivron said, pointing to the hole that Norris was clambering out of. The architect jumped down into the foundation pit and pulled Norris out of the hole he'd fallen into. He shone a torch down. The sarcophagus was just visible. Elaborate stone carvings were made into the side of it, the torchlight glinting off the relief. 'That's not a pit,' Chivron said, looking back to Peters. 'It's a burial crypt. The likes of which I've never seen.'

'Does this change much?' Norris asked.

'Potentially everything,' Chivron said. 'I wonder whose crypt it is. Scaliterri'd know.'

'Don't bother with him,' Peterson said. 'I've already arranged for a guy I know. He's going to blow it all up at the end of next week.'

'What? Are you mad, Peterson?' Chivron hissed. 'We can't just blow this up, Scaliterri would have a field day.'

'Scaliterri'll keep quiet if he knows what's good for him. May I remind you, Herve, of what's at play on this one. This is no playground. Now, please, pipsqueak, would you get out of that hole and stop making things worse?'

Norris shrugged, ascending the ladder. Peterson gave a filthy glare and turned his back on Norris, but the young man had a glance at Chivron's face. He was pensive.

The car ride back was silent. To break the silence which hung in the atmosphere of Norris' new Marina, he reached for the radio. His fingers encircled the knob. But another hand snapped it away.

'Don't,' Chivron said.

'You think he's really going to blow that away?'

'I hope not,' Chivron said. 'But he gets his way. Like Ballard. I still can't believe you didn't take that offer.'

'All flash, that. What I do means something,' Norris said. He smiled just a little. There was more to it than that, but that was too tawdry to discuss with his boss. 'Do you want him to?'

'No, but there's nothing I can do. There's more that drives this project than good intentions, Norris. Money. Power. And you know who'll be the scapegoat if it all goes wrong?'

'Peterson?'

Chivron laughed. 'No, I wish, Me. My legacy. This changes a lot, Norris. Regardless, the Tower's going to get built on a burial site. An important one, probably. I just can't see this going right. It has to, Norris, it's about bloody time it did. For me, the firm. For us.'

'I see,' Norris said, driving on and letting a man he respected enough to turn down a job at Ballard for a lot more money ponder on this fresh development.

Midnight. Norris fidgeted in his bed, awake, but his eyes were clamped shut.

Around him, in a swirl of colours. The world disappeared into nothingness.

He opened his eyes. This wasn't home. It wasn't even the city. Or the Nineteen Seventies. The vista he observed was green rolling hills under a grey, cloudy sky. Okay, maybe not too far from home, he thought. It was still just as cold as it was back home.

Back home, wherever that is.

He walked forward toward the hill. The ground was soft, like it'd recently rained. The air certainly smelled like it did when it rained. A pure scent. Not unpleasant.

Norris continued down the path toward a crop of woodland that sprouted like moss from the expanse of green. He stopped. Beyond the wood was the wisps of smoke.

Smoke meant fire. And fire meant people. The woody, warm smell wrapped up his nostrils. They wrinkled.

'What is this place?' he said, the syllables stolen by the breeze.

Sound came from behind one of the undulating mounds of green earth that formed the countryside. Birds scurried in a cluster of squawks. Over the hill, a figure emerged on horseback. Another came, and another, until a dozen or so other men riding on brown and grey steeds gathered. The lead man pointed right to Norris. The horse whinnied and reared, and the group of horsemen gave chase.

Norris wasn't going to stick around, and he turned and ran toward the wood. They couldn't follow him there. Norris didn't get far, tumbling quickly on the long, wet grass with a squeal. He turned, nursing a grazed knee. His pyjama trousers were stained green from the wet, wild grass.

The horsemen approached at a canter. Norris submitted, holding up his hands in the universal way of surrender.

'I give up, I give up!' he wailed. His head darted. All the horsemen wore rough leather and furs. The horses heaved and panted. The people on them murmured. Dirty faces obscured by beards and whiskers. The lead man jumped down from his horse.

'You not from here?' the horseman said.

'No-no, I don't know where I am. Who are you?'

'Drest. You Norman?'

'No, Norris. Stephen Norris,' Norris said. Blank looks radiated back. Norris gestured to himself. 'Nor-ris. From London.'

'He's Roman, probably,' one of the other horseman murmured into Drest's ear. Drest turned back to Norris.

'You go see Bran,' he said. 'He know what to do.'

Norris sighed. Bran sounded normal.

Bran was not normal. They'd hauled Norris onto one of their horses and taken him along a cobbled path to a large circular hut formed of low stone walls and a conical thatched roof. Smoke rose slowly from the centre of this construction. Drest hauled Norris equally firmly from the horse he'd carried him on.

'You wait here,' Drest spat. 'Bran important man. You wait.'

'Where are we?' Norris said with a shiver. The hut in front of him looked warm. Anything looked warm to him now.

'You not speak,' Drest said, leaning in. Norris could smell his fetid breath.

Norris nodded, the only motion he could muster. His pyjamas had been torn and were now filthy in mud and muck. Drest pushed back a curtain of loose fabric that led into the hut. He emerged a few moments later.

'You, in.'

One of the other horsemen pushed Norris inside. As the gloom of the building's interior scooped away daylight, he gasped.

In the middle of the space was a campfire that burned orange-red with flecks of yellow in the flames. On the opposite side against the wall an impressive wooden chair filled by an even more impressive man clad in the same studded leather and sporting a bushy, unkempt beard.

Norris knew this was Bran before he'd even been introduced, but Drest did so anyway, pushing Norris down in front of the imposing position Bran sat in, slightly raised and looking down on this strange captive. The heat of the fire behind bore down on Norris' back, the cold from outside now filled with beads of sweat.

'Norris,' Bran said.

'You know my name?'

'I know many things. You are not from this world, are you, boy?'

'I'm not. You speak better than the others.'

'I carry knowledge from the gods,' Bran said. Norris accepted it, unable to refuse. 'You come from a bleak and torturous future where roads are paved with stone and tar.'

'Er,' Norris thought, then realised. 'In a manner of speaking, yes. I don't know how I got here.'

'I commanded it, from prayers to the gods themselves.' Norris blinked. 'Turn and face the flame,' Bran boomed. Norris did so and Bran walked around. 'The flames, they talk of a dark future for my clan. My people. It will turn our legacy to ash and dust.'

'I see.'

'You can stop this. You have one mighty chance to stop this before my resting place and that of my people, is destroyed.'

'You... the one in the crypt?'

'Not far from here, we have built a stout stone room into which the gods may protect our mortal remains once we ascend. This stone room will stand for a thousand years. In the soil, in the rain, but it will remain in the world. Follow.'

Bran got up and Drest dragged Norris to his feet. They went outside, back into the cold. Already Norris was disappointed.

Beyond, Bran indicated to a rectangular object a couple of hundred metres away.

'Is that where we're going?'

'Does it scare you?'

'Everything scares me now.'

'Come,' Bran said, walking down the path.

Norris followed–with Drest's persuasion–Bran into the stone room dug into the valley floor. He took a sharp intake of breath.

The views from the building site came into clarity under the licking flames of torches–the reliefs on the walls, even the open sarcophagus.

'This is where I will lie once my mortal form passes,' Bran said. 'For a thousand years the gods will slumber with me.'

Norris looked around. He ran a hand down the smooth stone of the sarcophagus. He'd never feel this again. When he'd seen it earlier–or later, however this worked–the winds of time would chip it to lose its lustre. He turned around to look at Bran, Drest, and a handful of the others. 'How can I help you?'

Bran laughed. 'Push the right parchment, is that the role you lead?'

'I feel like I am coming up against God himself.'

'Himself?' Bran asked. 'Oh, yes. We have many gods. They can assist you.'

'How? I don't have to start praying, do I?'

Bran knelt down and smiled. He tapped his temple. 'You, Stephen Norris, have the power of the gods inside you, you just don't know it yet.' Norris opened his mouth to protest but Bran hushed him with his palm. 'You have a choice to make: save our mortal bones and the spirits they contain and we can reward you with the secrets of our gods, the true ones. If you fail, that spirit will infest your world.'

'Is there another way?'

'The will of the gods will be done one way or the other. Us mortals, even high elders like me, we are slaves to the will of the gods.'

Norris looked to the floor. He scooped up some of the dirt, letting it fall through his fingers. 'I suppose I must do my best.'

'You have powerful friends who can help you, you just need to piece it together, little Norris,' Bran said.

'I think I can,' Norris said. 'How do I get home?' Bran chuckled and reached for a flask on his belt. He pulled it away and offered it to Norris. 'What's in this?'

'A stout liquid. We won't meet again, Stephen Norris, not like this.'

Norris took a deep breath before he glugged down the liquid straight from the bladder. Immediately he felt his head gain weight, and the urge to sleep became uncontainable. Darkness filled his eyes, and the sound turned to a light buzzing.

He opened his eyes. It was morning, and he was in his bed, but drenched in sweat. That couldn't be, could it? He shook his head and threw the duvet aside. Norris glanced down, and what he saw stole the breath from his chest.

His pyjamas were ruined, covered in grass and mud, and his hands had left mucky handprints all over the cotton sheets.

After dressing, he routed through the box room he lived in, looking for the little book he knew was there somewhere. He found the little leather-bound book and palmed through, smiling. Norris hoped the number he dialled hadn't changed and put the book by the side of his bed.

He'd see if there was an answer later that evening.

'Great, see you soon,' Norris said, placing the receiver toward the holder.

He stepped out of the red telephone box and into the cool autumn evening and walked back up the road toward his house. The door clicked behind him.

'You're out late,' Norris' father said from the hallway.

'It's work, really,' Norris countered.

'Watch it, son, your tea's getting cold.'

Norris smiled. 'What're we having?'

His father smiled back. 'Captain Birdseye's finest.'

A couple of hours later, Norris emerged from the house. Wrapped up in a big coat, his breath formed cool clouds. The weather was turning chillier by the day. The usual space in the street outside was empty, for he had parked down the road. He clipped the car key to the Marina from under his coat and unlocked the car with a slow, careful turn of his wrist. The lock clicked once. He slipped in. The engine rattled, not liking the cold either. With a shudder and a splutter, two discs of yellow-white light illuminated the tarmac and Norris drove away. It was a ten-minute journey. He arrived at the empty, dark office first, then retraced his steps from his trip with Mr Chivron. A few more minutes later, he parked up just around the corner from a building site he'd become strangely familiar with despite only being there once.

Tonight was the second date.

Norris got out, back into the cold. He rubbed his hands together, then cocooned his face, blowing hard. The street was empty. The houses sheltered only ghosts behind the chipboard hoardings. They'd be cleared away next, once the Tower glistened above them. Norris checked his watch, the milky light from a streetlight reflecting on the cloudy glass.

'Come on, Adam,' he hissed to nobody.

Then came footsteps. Norris pivoted. A dark, tall figure cloaked in shadows approached. Norris took a sudden dislike to dark, tall figures around here and dove into a doorway of an condemned house.

The man walked slowly past, right to the spot that Norris had been in.

'Jesus, make me come all this way...' the shrouded man heaved. Norris smiled, emerging from the doorway.

'Hello trouble,' he said warmly. The man turned, then smiled back.

'Bastard! What're you doing hiding in the shadows?'

'You should see what I have to work with! Did you bring the...'

'I did,' Adam said, patting a shoulder bag. Something inside rattled. 'Shall we?'

'Yes, lets,' Norris said then turned, facing the hoarding that dominated the other side of the street. The pair made a beeline for the gate. It was open. Norris pushed it. The gate squealed, as if it were in pain from the motion. He winced. Adam did too.

'Careful,' Adam said, looking around. Houses surrounded the site, with not a light on. Nobody had been home for some time. 'Don't want to wake the neighbours.'

Norris stifled a laugh. He led Adam onto the site, which was a vista of total darkness. Norris glanced to the left as he entered.

'Shit!' he said. Almost total darkness. In the shack that served as the site office, the subtle glow of an electric light diffused through threadbare net curtains.

Adam froze, but Norris didn't. 'What are you doing?!' Adam asked, his voice calling toward Norris, who was opening the gap.

'I need to see,' Norris said, sneaking with careful, gazelle-like motions across the loose dirt and gravel that covered the site. It was like treading on muddy, orange snow, the sound of the particles compacting ringing out in the night's silence. Adam followed until they were at the threshold. Norris hugged the wall and slid along the rough-sawn timber of the side of the shed. He inched an eye through the glass, through the net curtain. Norris immediately folded back, almost hitting the wooden wall but stopping himself just before.

'What?' Adam mouthed. Norris shook his head and darted away from the shack. Once the pair were about twenty feet away Norris lent in toward his friend.

'It's him, he's sat there dozing in front of the telly!' Norris said, relating the scene of Peters, asleep in a chair, his feet propped up on a desk with the BBC close-down test card beaming from a little portable television in silence. A handful of empty brown beer bottles had festooned the desk. Clearly Peterson was working late this evening.

'Let's be quick,' Adam said. 'Lead the way.'

Norris did so, retracing his steps to the excavation in the middle of the site, the disc of light from the torch bouncing around the undulating mounds of raw earth. A noise from behind him made him twist. The torch danced around.

'Careful, for god's sake!' Norris hissed, seeing Adam propping up a wheelbarrow that had been left in the way.

'You should've told me to bring a torch!'

'I thought we'd only need one!' Norris countered, then stopped at the edge of the hole in the ground. Adam joined him. Norris pointed the torch down to the deeper hole where the cave in had taken place.

'Did your fat arse do that?' Adam said.

Norris sighed. 'Get down that hole.'

Adam knelt and twisted, positioning himself on the ladder into the rough pit. He scraped down the ladder, followed by Norris, who tiptoed in front of him.

'Why'd I get the idea we could get in a lot of trouble...' Adam begun.

Norris hushed him. 'Get the ladder,' he said. Adam picked it up and dragged it with a staccato scrape that ruffled the loose dirt. 'Quietly!' Adam picked it up and carried it, placing it gently into the hole. Adam turned, ready to descend again. Norris passed him the torch.

'Ready to descend into hell?' Norris said, smiling wickedly.

'Button it, Steve,' Adam said back, sliding down the ladder with a swish, his feet hitting the floor with a distant thud.

'Adam?' Norris called with his hands cupped around his hands.

'This is unreal, Steve,' Adam said in a hoarse whisper. 'We never thought places like this existed.'

'What're you saying?'

'Look,' Adam said, throwing the light up to a far wall away from the ladder. Carvings into the very stone of the wall depicted people, some with grotesque and amazing features. Adam highlighted a serious-looking visage of a man with a flowing, unkempt beard and two curled horns emerging from his temples. '*Cernunnus*,' he muttered. 'The horned one.'

'I was right to call you.'

'And look,' he continued, '*Alator*, the god of war. And *Brigit*, too, look,' he breathed, illuminating the worn but unmistakable features of a warrior woman formed of solid stone. But his genuine awe was swept away by the monument in the middle of the space. 'This is incredible. What did you say they were going to do?'

'Blow it up on Wednesday and fill it with cement.'

'Oh goodness me, no,' Adam inhaled sharply. 'That can't be allowed.'

'It can't be stopped either. Got any ideas?'

'We thought a crypt was somewhere in this area, I'll have to check the records at the office, but this may indeed be it. The lost crypt of St. Brigit, lost all this time.' Adam trailed off, opening his bag. He pulled out the Polaroid camera and began snapping.

Norris swallowed. 'Can we, well...'

'Move any of this? No, this needs to be saved. Preserved. This could be worth millions of pounds, Steve.'

'Let's get out of here,' Norris suggested. 'We'll talk tomorrow.'

'Sounds good,' Adam said, following his friend to the ladder. Norris clambered up, stopping dead still halfway. 'What?'

Norris slid back down. 'We've got company, Adam. They're coming this way.'

'What do you mean?' Adam said, scrambling toward the ladder. Norris held him back.

'Wait.' Norris climbed the ladder slowly, one rung at a time, pushing himself up. He checked first, before hauling himself out of the crypt and into the rest of the foundation footing. He waved Adam up. He followed. 'Now carefully,' Norris said in barely a whisper, 'get the ladder and stick it over there,' he pointed to the edge of the pit.

Adam nodded and did so, pulling at the metal ladder with precision. He swung it around in, placing it ever so slowly against the edge of the pit.

'I'll go, then you follow,' Norris said. He climbed up the ladder, even more slowly and quietly than before. He stopped with his head just shy of the rim of the pit. Norris swallowed. Beyond the pit, toward the gate, a carmine-coloured Ford Transit stood facing toward the office. In the gloom he made out two letters stencilled onto the side panel.

'Who's D. W?' Adam asked.

'Dunno, but I don't like the look of that.'

The van rocked irregularly. A man was unloading it, with another man watching, holding the lead to a large dog that looked like a Doberman. It panted in clouds of breath.

Norris vaulted out of the pit and scarpered toward the hoarding at the edge of the site that was shrouded in total darkness. He backed into it, then indicated to Adam to do the same.

What?! Adam mouthed.

Come here! Norris said back wordlessly. Adam nodded, taking a deep breath and vaulting himself out of the pit. The loose ground crunched, and Adam belted it across the site.

Norris's eyes tracked to movement in the pit. The ladder was falling backwards - hitting the bottom of the pit with a clatter.

The Transit stopped rocking instantly.

'Hey, who made that racket?' a raspy voice called.

'Wasn't me!' another replied.

'Peterson, you twat, you said it was just us!' the first voice added.

'It is! Go check it out,' a familiar voice grated through the air: the gravelly intonations of Peterson.

'Alright, alright,' a third voice sighed. 'Come on, boy.'

Boy? Norris thought then remembered: the Doberman. A panting and pawing sound filtered through the air. From behind the van, a torch emerged, and sharp teeth glistened in the moonlight. Norris wasn't planning on staying around to be the dog's dinner, and ran at full pelt toward the yard entrance, stopping halfway there. He turned around. 'Adam, move!'

Adam ran behind. The skidding gravel kicked up a racket of scratchy, scraping stones that was impossible to ignore: the disc of light from the man with the Doberman pivoted, shining on both Norris and Adam.

'Hey, you! You shouldn't be in here!' the man yelled from under his cagoule, jogging toward them. The Doberman barked hoarsely, growling, straining at its lead.

'Sod this,' Adam yelled, sprinting toward the yard entrance.

'Get the gate!' the pursuer yelled as well.

'Shit!' Norris hissed, keeping tandem with Adam. The gate was just a few feet away, one of the men rushing to pull it closed. Norris jumped, rolling around the gate just as it swept closed with a loud thundering clatter. He looked over his shoulder to Adam.

'Quick, Steve!'

Norris pulled on the gate. It didn't open. Grasping at the metal, he pulled. His eyes clamped shut with the effort. Then the gate fell to the ground in a shower of golden sparks.

'Where'd the hell that come from?!' Adam heaved, scampering over the gate.

Norris took a deep, harsh breath of night air. 'My car!' he said, turning as Adam ran past. The man with the Doberman sped out of the compound.

'Come 'ere ya gits,' he rattled as the Doberman barked.

Norris thumped into the side of the Marina, fumbling for the key. It jittered into the lock, then turned. The door clicked open. He fell in. Two hands banged on the opposite glass.

'Let me in!' Adam shouted; his voice muffled by the glass. Norris leant over and released the catch. Adam tumbled into the car. 'Get us outta here!'

In the rear-view mirror, the man with the Doberman was just thirty feet away. Norris pushed the key into the ignition and turned. The Marina slumped forward, but the engine didn't crank. Norris tried again. The car didn't crank a second time. 'Please,' he pleaded, just under his breath, turning the key a third time. The Leyland engine under the bonnet spluttered to life, just as the man with the Doberman slapped a palm on the back quarter of the car.

'Go!' Adam shouted.

'Alright!' Norris countered, putting his foot down and, with a squeal of rubber on a worn asphalt road, the Marina carried them away.

She rapped on the old, battered wooden door as the autumn wind threatened to carry her away. On the other side, metallic rattling. Then the door thrust roughly open.

'Huh,' an old, grizzly faced man grunted. 'You want?'

'Oh, hello,' Deborah started. 'Are you Bill Baxter?' The man already started to close the door. 'Wait! You knew my dad, Tim Wrenly.'

The man in the doorway paused. His mouth fell agape. 'Tim Wrenly, now that's a name I've not heard in many a year. Come in, girl, it's too bloody cold for you to stand on your feet in the wind.'

Deborah crossed the threshold into the cramped little house. Pots and pans piled high on the kitchen sides. She edged through, as the man indicated out of the kitchen into the front room. Deborah entered, seeing a crusty old lady in an armchair regarding her severely.

'Tim Wrenly's little girl,' Bill grunted. The old woman thought for a moment.

'Nice lad, Tim was. How's he?'

'Fine,' Deborah said. Bill waved at his wife.

'Go make some tea, woman,' he said. She got up, her hips creaking. 'This ain't a social call, is it, young Deborah?'

'You remember my name.'

'I do. How is your dad doing?'

'Alright, considering...'

'Yes,' Bill hummed. 'Considering.'

'I wondered if you could help. Back in the day, you knew

some characters.'

Bill chuckled. 'I'll say. Back when we were up chimneys hanging by a piece of thread.'

'Right, you see... if you wanted to blow something up, what would you use?'

Bill's eyebrows rose. 'German bridges?'

'No, in the trade.'

'Ah yes, sorry. To build you must destroy. That was what our job was. Pulling down chimneys. Watching them blast away. It was a life, until...' he trailed off, his gaze falling to his gammy leg. 'There's a story to this, isn't there?'

Deborah nodded and explained. Bill wheezed, getting up and moving to an ancient and collapsing cabinet. He opened one of the doors with a wail and rooted about inside. Deborah spied through the corner of her eye the piles of loose and disorganised paper. A microcosm of the rest of this house, as the living room was, too, piled high with ancient junk.

'Aha!' Bill called and thrust a note of paper into Deborah's hand.

'Who's *D. W.*?' she asked.

'Davey Whelan, the only person your man would possibly be dealing with. Big bang with no paperwork? Easy, call Dave.'

'I'll go see him.'

'That's his house. Not where he keeps the stuff. At least, I hope not. I'd hate to live down his street when it gets rowdy.'

Deborah pocketed the paper and got up. 'Thanks.'

'I'll show you out, then,' Bill wheezed once more. He led Deborah to the kitchen door. 'Maybe one day I'll see your dad again, just like old times.'

'Maybe,' she said.

'Be careful when you meet Whelan, he's slipperier than a sack of eels,' Bill said.

'Thank you.'

'Well, goodbye. And good luck helping your young man.'

The door closed and Deborah walked toward the bus stop but pivoted at the corner of the road. Instead, she turned, getting on the bus away from home but toward the address on the slip of yellowed paper offered to her by Bill Baxter. The bus soon approached, and she hopped on, like Norris had done, and offered her coins to the conductor in exchange for a slip of card giving her carriage.

The bus turned through the rapidly encroaching night past shops and into an eerie industrial district. Workmen clambered on the bus, leering at Deborah in her pretty coat.

'Alright darlin'!'

'Fancy a bit o' ruff?!'

She shook her head meekly, eventually dinging the bell and alighting from the Routemaster. She took a few steps down the cracked pavement, losing herself in a tawdry, overgrown industrial estate. The street-lamps were fizzling on one by one, illuminating the street with a chemical orange.

The shabby unit Deborah had looked for soon loomed around a corner, nearly completely shrouded by wild, unkempt shrubs and bushes that pushed through the lousy dirt. It was dilapidated and ancient, the asbestos roof panels cracked and askew atop worn concrete and brickwork. A door toward the front looked piled high with parts and junk, as were the two windows that flanked it. Beyond, a dim but present glow showed that there was life.

Deborah skipped the front door and slid down the alleyway to the side that was just wide enough. Her nose wrinkled. It stunk of piss and chemicals. She trod lightly, hardly able to see. The alleyway opened to a cramped yard, which was also filled with junk: wrecks of cars and their innards and desiccated packaging torn apart by the elements.

A door in the building's side was open. Deborah poked her head around the threshold. The inside of the warehouse was as equally dilapidated as the outside, except for some packages.

These looked brand new, almost pristine but for some grubby fingerprints on the white, neatly folded cardboard. Some were open, exposing pearly-paper around a glistening substance.

Deborah leant in. The scent of chemicals was stronger with every move she made. She stepped forward, trying to read the printed text on the cardboard.

Danger - high explo

'What're you doin' here?' a voice growled from behind. Deborah yelped. She saw the shape of the man in the gloom, a pair of glowing eyes staring at her from the darkness. Jolting back, she dislodged a piece of metal from its resting place against the door frame and it hit the cement floor with a clang.

'Sorry, I think, I don't know...'

'Get out of here, or I'll have to eat that pretty face of yours,' the figure leered forward. Deborah backed into the actual warehouse space. The shadow followed, revealing a gristly, dirty man under a sodden mac. He smiled, exposing crooked, chipped teeth.

'Who are you?'

'Why does someone so pretty want to know? You're lost, little girl. Want me to find you?'

'No!' Deborah spat back. 'Whelan, right?'

'Depend's who's askin".

'I am, that's all you need to know.'

'You ain't a customer and you ain't gonna be. So forget you were here and piss off back to your fairytale castle.'

Deborah retreated past Whelan's form and out of the yard, past the dirty, crimson Transit that was parked in the yard.

Inside, Whelan laced his filthy fingers around a dirty plastic phone on the wall and dialled. A voice picked up.

'Did he come?' the voice rattled.

'No, but a girl did.'

The voice laughed. 'Close enough.'

In the upstairs bedroom, Clive and Pat Norris snoozed. Clive fidgeted. Something outside was making him stir. Opening his eyes, somehow the sound from outside filtered through with more clarity.

Tinkling like that of glass. Grunts of effort. And rhythmic thudding, with the crumpling of plate.

Clive growled. They were awake now and hoisted himself out of bed to the window. A sleepy hand pushed the net curtain aside. It was pouring outside, the rain clattering against the glass. A wind rattled the window in the frame. But in the gloom two figures were walking away from the house, down the road opposite, their dark figures dissolving into the darkness.

'Come back to bed,' Pat murmured. Clive turned around, grunting himself. He clambered back into the warm comfort of the bed and dozed off, not giving the two figures another moment's thought - they had already disappeared from his mind.

'You're going to be late for work, Stephen,' Clive said, hearing the feet clatter down the stairs. Norris emerged into the kitchen-diner and stole a piece of toast from his father's plate. 'Oi!'

'Sorry dad,' Norris said. 'Needs must.'

'If you got up earlier-'

'See you dad! And you, mum,' Norris said. He leant in to kiss his expectant mother on the cheek. 'I've got to pick Deborah up.'

'You like her, don't you?'

Norris paused in the doorway to the hall. He let a smile percolate across his face. 'I think I do, Dad.'

Clive smiled and gestured with a flick of his neck toward the front door. 'Get out there, son.' The door clicked closed. 'She's a nice girl, that Deborah,' he started toward Pat. A scream broke the conversation. 'What on earth?'

The front door banged open. Norris emerged into the kitchen again, wheezing. 'Dad!'

'What's happened?'

'My car! My wonderful car!'

Clive leapt to his feet and followed his son out of the kitchen, through the living room and out into the damp street. He proceeded down the little front path to the kerb. What greeted him made his jaw drop. 'My god.'

The Marina was smashed to hell. Shards of glass hung in the window. The metal bodywork was dented and the tyres all flat against the asphalt.

'Who did this?' Pat said, following her husband out.

'I thought I heard something last night,' Clive admitted.

Norris glared. 'And you didn't look?!'

'It was pouring! And I couldn't see anyone. Thought I saw a couple of figures though but that might've been some trick of the night.'

Norris swallowed, feeling his stomach collapse. 'I think it might be more than that.'

'Oh, Stephen,' Pat said. 'This isn't a work thing, is it?'

'It might be,' Norris said. He glanced into the wrecked car. The interior was just as trashed as the exterior, the seats ripped and stuffing poking out of the wounds. But propped up on the dash in front of the steering wheel was a square of glossy paper. Opening the door, Norris reached in. He took the piece of paper. Glancing at it, his stomach somersaulted again.

It was Norris in front of this very car. Clive took the photo from Norris.

'That's the photo we took in the summer. How did they get this?'

'It was at work,' Norris said. 'In my office. On the pin board.'

Clive turned the Polaroid over. On the back were words scrawled in dirty black pen. 'You were warned, now stay out of the dirt unless you want to be buried,' he read.

'Peterson,' Norris said. 'He must've seen me and Adam when we...'

'When you what, Stephen?' Norris looked to the ground.

'What did you do?'

Norris told the story, in abbreviated terms.

'Bold, but foolish,' Clive said.

'Oh, Stephen,' his mother cooed. 'What a thing to be dragged into.'

In the distance at the bottom of the road, the Routemaster bus turned the corner. 'Gotta go, mum and dad.'

'Now, wait a mo,' Clive started but Norris was already out of the garden and across the street toward the bus stop.

'Deborah! Call Deborah! I'll get the bus to work, hopefully she's alright!'

The bus gave a throaty roar of its engine as Norris hopped on the open platform at the back.

'Tickets,' the conductor droned. Norris shoved a penny into the man's hand. He wound the ticket machine and it spat out a paper ticket. The bus lurched and Norris tumbled from the staircase into the upper saloon. If only he had a phone in his pocket, he thought. But such things were in the land of make-believe, and all he could do was wait for the bus to snake through the morning traffic and hope Deborah was alright.

Norris fell through the office door and glanced at the clock on the wall. The maroon second hand swept past ten-seventeen. Then his head came down. 'Deborah,' he beathed. 'You're alright.'

'Better than you are!' she said. 'What happened to you?'

'No time to explain, has-'

She glanced to the ceiling. 'Here bright and early. Has something happened, you look a wreck...'

'Not now,' Norris waved. He stumbled over to his desk, pulling open the drawers. They were just as chaotically packed as Norris had left them, so he couldn't tell readily if they'd been ransacked. But the Polaroid in the ruins of his car had been enough. They'd been here when they shouldn't have been. He'd been here. He'd been to his house. In the dead of night. 'I'm going up,' Norris said.

'Please, Steve, don't do anything stupid!'

'Deborah, nothing matters more than what I am about to do.' He leant in and pecked her on the cheek, then strode through the back door of the office and up the stairs. His feet thudded as he raced up, skipping every other tread in his haste. He grasped the office door and flung it open. Peters and Chivron were there, both caught out by the energy with which Norris had opened the door.

'You.'

'Ah,' Peterson said suavely, 'Mr Norris. You weren't in when I came in to discuss the particulars of the removal of the crypt with Mr Chivron here-'

'You know damn well why I wasn't here, you bastard.'

'Whoa, Stephen,' Chivron said quickly, waving in protest. 'There's no need for that!'

Norris took a big gasp of air. He was still on an adrenalin high and recouping from running up those damn stairs. His eyes flickered, settling in Chivron for a moment, then fixing a gaze back on Peters. 'Yes there is. You were here last night. Then you were at my house. What was that meant to be, some kind of scare tactic?'

Peterson gave a confused look which hardened into a glare. 'We don't all come out of this squeaky clean, pipsqueak. Where were you on Friday night then? Poking around where you shouldn't be, that's where. Trespassing on site. Nearly broke your neck in the hole, again.'

'Would someone please explain to me,' Mr Chivron began calmly, his voice rising, 'what the hell is going on here?!'

'He,' Norris pointed to Peterson, gasping for breath, 'paid a late-night visit to my house. He trashed my car. Or one of your little lackeys did.'

'You were poking around the site again after hours! You and that weird friend of yours, nearly got yourselves killed and for what?'

'Killed? I was showing him what you were planning on blowing up, you won't do it, you know. I won't let you. You can't, not once you see-'

'What, are a load of old bones going to wake up and scare me at Halloween? Please, you don't know what you're dealing with, you little squirt...'

Norris took a breath but noticed Chivron had turned a plum red. He held in his words, letting Peterson carry on ranting.

'Will you two please shut the hell up?!' Chivron boomed. The silence that followed acted like a thousand pinpricks on the back of Norris' neck. 'Norris, what you did was silly, sites are dangerous enough as it is.'

'You didn't see what else I saw,'

'What's that?' Chivron said, leaning back in his chair.

'Careful, boy,' Peterson growled. Chivron shut him down with a glance of iron.

'That shack office is stacked full of explosives. He was having his poodles unload it in the middle of the night. Surprised you didn't blow your own damn face off.'

'I wish I'd blown yours off instead,' Peters grumbled. Chivron waved.

'What do you mean he was unloading the explosives? For a demolition? I thought things had been agreed, we were going to see how things panned out. I *hope* this is all above-board, Peterson, or does your reputation precede you once again?'

'I don't like your tone, Herve.'

'I'm not asking you to.'

'Enough. This is how they're going to pan out,' Peterson began, standing up. 'There's too much money at stake. You know that, I know that. This is all a sideshow. Mysterious crypts and pretend gods. It's standing in our way and I, and the people I really work for, just won't put up with it.'

'Will you at least hear out the reasons why this really shouldn't be what you're doing, please?' Norris said.

'No, I shan't. The decision has been made, right at the very top. Oh, and I think I know who you were with, pipsqueak. Scaliterri's boy. Another do-gooder. Should I visit him, too?'

'No!'

'Then behave. You know, we really don't need you to finish the Tower. You have been most kind, Mr Chivron, to provide the plans and drawings well in advance. My team can complete it.'

'Don't do this, Peterson, please, this doesn't have to be the way our partnership ends.'

'But don't blow it up, try to save some of the legacy from the crypt at least,' Norris said. Peters laughed. 'Do you want this to be your legacy? Destroying an important historical site to throw up a tower block?'

'Careful, Norris,' Chivron said.

'But it's true! Have you met with Mr Scaliterri, he's fascinating. And he, along with me, it seems, is the only one that cares! Look,' Norris said, seeing Chivron shrivel up in his chair, 'the Tower bears your name. Do you want your legacy to be that of obliterating history - and not just that, people died there, people we don't even know! It's like bulldozing a cemetery to put a car park there, not knowing what's there beforehand. Imagine paving over the bones of the King of England to park your car? Don't you want to know at least before you make a terrible mistake?' Norris breathed heavily.

'You finished?' Peterson asked. 'That was a nice speech. But it means nothing. It's a load of old shit. If the King of England is in that crypt, or Boudicca or whoever, they're getting turned to dust. The future is now, and we need to fix the problems this town and city has today. The real powers that be, and I know them, and you, Herve—they'd want it this way. I am as powerless as you to save this thing. This is why I'm expediting the process.'

Chivron have a single humourless laugh. 'Peterson, if I didn't know you better, I'd say that was the most... philanthropic thing you've ever said. If I didn't know you even better than that, I'd almost believe it was true.'

'Laugh all you want, you pair of little toerags, we'll be blasting that crap out and getting on with the work this week.' Peters looked past Norris. 'This is your final warning, Herve. I'll keep you in the loop, but your puppy,' he said, poking Norris in the ribs, 'comes within a hundred feet of my site again and we're finished. Done.' Norris gulped. Peterson then turned to him. 'Are you getting the picture now? You want to save the old man's legacy? Butt out. Unless you want your friend to get a visit too? Or maybe that delightful piece of skirt downstairs.'

'You leave her out of this,' Norris said, lunging forward. Peters backed away and laughed.

'The decision's up to you now, pipsqueak.' He opened the door. 'Friday, I reckon we'll blast through the trouble we've had, eh Herve?'

Norris glanced from Peters to Chivron. 'Just go,' the old man said, waving the council employee away. 'Get out for now, I've too much to take in.'

Peters left without another word. Norris paced around the office for a few seconds, shaking.

'Sit down,' Chiron spat. Norris did so. His mouth fell open as he went to speak, but Chivron held up a hand. 'Before you say a word, I know.'

'Know what?'

'I spoke to Scaliterri over the weekend. It seems Mr Peterson's renegade actions have not been unnoticed.'

'There must be some checks and balances for this.'

'The only checks, it would seem, are cheques. But I realise the importance of the site. Your little expedition,' he chuckled. 'In my youth I'd have done much the same thing. Did you bring the photographs?'

'No,' Norris said.

'No matter. This places us at a crossroads of sorts. My legacy is ruined whatever happens.'

'What do you mean?'

'A failed architect destined to design crummy shacks for the rest of his days or one so spectacularly egotistical to blow up a priceless antiquity to, as you put it, throw up some council flats. I've got to decide which fate I consign myself to.'

There was silence. Then Norris spoke. 'You can make the best crummy shacks anyone's ever seen. But you're not even doing the demolition, why is this on you?'

'Before you joined, I wanted a pinnacle. A magnum opus, if you will. Chivron Tower will be that, one way or the other. Peterson,' Chivron continued, seeing Norris' curious gaze, 'has the handy cloak of being from the local authority, it's like an anonymity we could all dream of. If only I'd not been so insistent earlier on. He'll easily want to pin any blowback on me and me alone, you see. Either way, Peters gets away scot-free, and I face the future one way or the other.'

'So you mean...'

'We've got a week to try to put some kind of stop to it. Scaliterri and your friend Adam are already on the way. But we'll need to be more discreet. Can you do that?'

Norris got up and went to leave. 'I reckon so. It's the right thing to do, even if it ruins us all.'

'Our legacy can be that of trying to do the right thing in the face of easier choices,' Chivron said as Norris stepped through the door. 'And Norris?'

'Yes?'

'I'm sorry about your car. Leave it with me.'

'You don't have to, sir.'

'I want to, alright.'

Norris smiled. 'Thank you, then.'

Norris, Adam and Deborah were the only passenger son the top deck of the bus that evening. They huddled at the rear of the upper saloon.

'Reckon he'll be there?' Adam asked.

'I hope not,' Deborah said. 'God, he was awful. He stunk.'

'Don't worry,' Norris said, grabbing her hand. 'We'll sort him.'

'What if that other guy's there?' Adam said. 'That Peterson guy?'

'Why would he be? Not like him to get his hands dirty,' Deborah said.

Norris hummed. 'I wouldn't put much past that git, you know. Whatever happens,' he took a deep breath, 'and however this ends, it is what it is.'

The bus lurched around a corner, the wind that propelled rain like spears of water at the metal sides rattling against the carriage. They were nearly there, and soon were deposited on that cold, grey and damp corner in an anonymous forest of industrial buildings.

'This way,' Deborah said, pulling her coat up tight. Norris shielded her with an umbrella.

'Sorry mate,' he said to Adam, who was without an umbrella. 'You'll have to make do.'

'Whatever I'm being paid, it's not enough,' Adam replied.

Norris laughed just once. 'Come on.'

They snaked through the sheds and warehouses that festooned this part of town. On one side of the road, the buildings petered out to a long fence, the base of which was shrouded with weeds and shrubs.

'This is it,' Deborah said, stopping on the corner opposite Whelan's filthy hovel of a building. The rain had slowed to a fine, cold mist that hissed in the air around.

'Can't see any lights,' Adam said. But Norris and Deborah had already crossed over the road. 'Wait!'

They entered the yard with trepidation. Deborah led the way until they reached the corner of the grubby little shack that led to the dark and dank alleyway.

'You want me to go first?' Norris asked. Deborah nodded. 'Okay. Adam,' he said over his shoulder. 'Keep an eye out.'

Norris took the first step, feeling a squelch under his shoe. His nose wrinkled as he entered the alleyway, the stench of ancient ammonia and stagnant water and goodness knows what other chemicals attenuated by the sheer sides of the walls either side. 'Christ,' he heaved. 'Anything?'

'No,' Adam said. 'Christ it stinks,'

'He's a filthy bastard, this guy, to the bone.'

Deborah shushed them as the sound of a diesel engine approached. They all froze. It could be the dirty rotten Transit. But the throaty gurgle disappeared as quickly as it came into the hissing precipitation.

Norris emerged from the alleyway into the rear yard. It was dim, no lights coming from any of the windows. 'Nobody home.'

'Good,' Adam said. 'That the door?'

'It is,' Deborah said, sidling up to the closed door that she'd had the misfortune of seeing open the previous night. Norris pushed it. It was firm.

'How do we get in,' he asked aloud. They backed away from the door and searched the yard.

'How about this?' Deborah said. Norris came over. She passed him a length of timber. Norris grabbed it, smiling at Deborah. The smile faded as he held the sodden wood in his hands. It was slimy, cold and filthy. He moved, pushing the wood under the lip of the door. Then he pushed. The door jittered.

'You sure that's going to do it?' Adam asked as the wood creaked.

'It has to, can't see any other way.'

'Nearly, Steve!' Deborah urged.

'Keep it down!' Adam said. Over his shoulder, another diesel engine rattled, closer and closer. 'Quickly, Steve.'

Norris pushed down on the length of wood, grunting with the effort. The door seemed to be moving more against its frame, like it wanted to be free. 'One more push, reckon we'll have gotten it,' he heaved. He felt a warmness in his arms. Knowing what it was, he smiled wickedly, then pushed down on the wooden beam.

The rattling of the diesel engine was now loudly on the other side of the yard gate. A door opened, then closed, in quick thud-thud succession. Then the chain on the other side of the gate that held the latch closed jingled with a metallic thrang. Adam moved past Norris and yanked on the door as Norris pushed down once more on the timber. It splintered, but the door that they were trying to force open cracked too as rusted bolts lost their bite on the old wood. With a crack and a hollow thud, the timber cracked, but the door stood ajar, leaking darkness from within.

'In!' Norris said. Deborah and Adam scampered toward the door, Norris being the last in, pulling it closed just as the gate creaked open and the lights of the crimson Transit illuminated the door, the dirty glow lighting up the back of the warehouse through the window at the top of the door. The engine roared and the motion cast the shadows of paint cans and tools into a weird dance across the wall.

'Christ, what sort of dump is this place?' Adam asked.

'Hide!' Norris said. 'It's him!'

The trio dashed around the space as the van parked up outside. The engine rattled to nothing once again.

'Hmm,' a voice called through the rain, through the ply of the shed door. 'Don't remember leavin' that here...'

The wood, Norris thought. It was discarded on the floor outside. The colour drained from his face. Outside, a bunch of keys jangled, but the door creaked open.

'Hey!' a gritty voice barked. 'Who's in my shop? Is it you, pretty little thing?'

Deborah grasped Norris' hand in a tight squeeze.

A switch flicked and a series of bare bulbs hanging from the ceiling fizzled into life. Behind the shelving unit, Norris, Deborah and Adam huddled, trying not to cough on the cloying vapour emanating from the old cans.

Whelan closed the door. The bolts that had hung on like rotten teeth fell out, tinkling onto the cement floor. He knelt, picking them up with his grubby fingers.

'You're here, aren't you, pretty little thing?' He sniffed hard. 'I know all the scents of this place, and yours is a new one.'

Behind the shelves, Norris nudged Deborah. *But all I can smell is old turps...*

'Out, the three of you,' Whelan said.

'What?!' Adam hissed. Then he looked past the shelves and saw the three shadows on the floor that had given them away.

'Out!' Whelan repeated. Adam was the first out, hands held above his head, knowing the game was up. 'And you two,' Whelan said, making a pulling motion with his hands. Norris followed, scowling at the grisly man. Then Deborah popped out of the hiding spot and into the open workshop. 'I was right, she is a pretty little thing, isn't she?'

Norris pushed forward toward Whelan. 'Keep your grubby mitts to yourself, you old bastard.'

'Explain yourself, boy. And you,' Whelan turned on the two young men. 'Pretty little thing, all you had to do was ask and ol' Whelan would've whisked you away.'

'Like hell you would!' Norris said again.

'Temper, temper,' Whelan said. 'He did warn me that you were quite the little pipsqueak. You shouldn't have brought her.' Whelan stopped pacing and looked at Deborah with deep regard. 'You keep bad company, pretty little-'

'Call her that again,' Norris lunged forward, 'and you'll be sorry.'

Whelan pushed Norris away. 'Be quiet. He never said you were this bolshy.'

'Who did?' Adam asked.

Whelan pivoted. 'Peterson. You, I wasn't warned about.' Whelan pointed to Adam. 'You seem sensible. No heroics.'

'We've come for the explosives. The stuff you're supplying to Peterson.'

Whelan held up his hands in mock protest. 'Innocent of all charges.'

'Don't be ridiculous. Deborah saw them last night.'

Whelan's eyes lit up and he grinned, showing his rotten teeth. 'She has a name! A pretty name, at that. How's that for you, *Debbie*!'

Norris sighed with regret at Whelan's display of palpable excitement. The bugger was practically drooling. His cheeks glowed. *Schoolboy error, Stephen.*

'Don't you dare call me Debbie. I saw the boxes on the bench over there,' Deborah said, thrusting her head toward the workbench. Four white cardboard boxes stood on it. 'Look, there it is.'

'That is none of your concern.'

'We know what you're going to blow up with it. Where did you get it?'

Whelan rolled his eyes. 'I'm not getting into this with you. Yes, it's for Peterson. Yes, it's to blow up the thing you fell into that's getting a lot of very important people very pissed off. Yes, he's paid me handsomely for it.'

Norris took a deep breath and then threw himself into something he'd regret. He tackled Whelan, pushing the old man to the ground, roaring with the motion. Whelan yelped, falling to the floor and skidding toward the bench, which teetered. 'Peterson!' Whelan yelled. 'Peterson, get in here!'

The door opened, letting in a gust of night air. A man emerged from the rainy gloom. Beyond that, flashing lights.

In emerged Peterson, accompanied by two policemen.

'I think we've found our three culprits trying to rob this innocent man,' Peterson said. 'Whelan, you doing alright?'

'You were right to warn me about this lot,' Whelan said. 'Nothing but trouble.'

'Will the stuff be ready for Thursday?'

'You said Friday!' Norris yelped.

'Button it, pipsqueak,' Peterson said. He turned back to Whelan. 'Well?'

'We should be ready, yes.'

'Excellent,' Peterson said. 'I'll leave you, then,' he said to Norris, 'in the hands of these fine gentlemen.'

The two policemen advanced and reached not for Whelan but for Norris and Adam. Deborah screamed like a banshee into the blue night sky, but it did no good.

Chivron unlocked the office as he did every morning and took a deep breath. The door sighed open too, and he stepped in.

The office was empty, but that wasn't unusual. Chivron was always the first here. Without fail. He paced through the office toward the rear corridor where the stairs to his office above were located. Placing a hand on the knob to that door leading to the back, he paused.

He felt a draft and looked down. The hems of his trousers were flapping.

Chivron felt his chest tighten. Internally he counted to five and pulled the door open. He stumbled back as the wind snapped the door against the wall and neutral and featureless sunlight greeted him.

This corridor didn't have a window.

He glanced to the left. The door to the outside alleyway was open.

Chivron turned right toward the stairs and went up them, with each step taking another breath in preparation for what he had an ominous inkling was to come.

'Hello, Herve,' Peterson said from Chivron's chair as the architect opened the door. Chivron let it slam behind him. 'You met Mr Townsend here,' Peterson shot a look to a lanky fellow beside him with a muddy face, 'on site recently.'

'Brought the builders in for me, then?' Chivron said.

'You wanna watch that mouth,' Townsend spat.

'Easy,' Peterson said with a gesture. 'Today's the day we get back on track.'

'If I recall, I'd fulfilled my end of the bargain. You and your team,' Chivron said slowly, 'had not.'

'Shall I?' Townsend said.

'Quiet,' Peterson commanded. He held his chest in mock outrage. 'You break my heart, Herve, are you not happy with the terms of our partnership?' Chivron went to speak but Peterson held up a dirty finger. 'Don't say it. I thought we, as gentleman, had an agreement on the problems we found.'

'We did, I've stuck to my word, much as I'll know I'll rue it very soon.'

'Have you? We've seen your associates. They've been causing us... issues, shall we say?'

'Issues?'

'Last night they were found trying to burgle a warehouse owned by a partner of mine, Damon Whelan. Name ring a bell?'

'Should it?'

'He was a licenced demolition expert.'

'Did he have an accident?'

'What?'

'You said he was licenced. You know what I'm getting at.'

'He's not dead,' Peterson sneered. 'He's just no longer licenced. Looks like your freaky friends were trying to make off with the good stuff. Stuff that I had paid good money for to do a job!'

Chivron laughed. 'Come off it, Peterson. Do you really think Norris and the others are that damn stupid?'

Peterson got up. 'Need I remind you that *pipsqueak*... Mr Norris, should I say, is one of the main reasons we are in this little predicament.'

'He didn't conjure the crypt into existence. That's preposterous.

You must've known it was there, but you kept me in the dark. How is this my fault?'

Peterson ignored the retort. 'But he has tried to make sure we can't magic 'em out of existence. I saw him and his friend on site, too. They were poking around where they shouldn't. Maybe I could ask the ol' bill to add trespass to the charge sheet.'

Chivron laughed. 'If any of this is true...'

'You'll see when he doesn't turn up this morning. Probably waking up under a bucket of ice right now. His parents'll kill him. Actually no,' Peterson said, gesturing again to his lad. 'You won't see them this morning.'

'Why?' Chivron asked. 'Ow!' he yelled, feeling Townsend grab his arms from behind.

'You're our guest of honour on site when we fix the mistakes the way we planned. Face it, Chivron, your honour has lost you this one. Maybe we'll let you keep the name on the Tower. You're the face of it, after all. I simply serve the Borough as a public servant.'

'You're a bastard, Peterson, and you're making a big mistake!'

'The only mistake we made was letting you know about all this. That's what courtesy gets you these days. You made the problem worse. Get your little bleeding heart of you and your little boy poking around.'

'Don't blame me for your failings as a contractor and, and... as a human being, you bastard! I should've known the moment I set eyes on you at that meeting you'd be trouble. The whole bloody lot of you stink!'

'Take him,' Peterson said to Townsend, and walked out of Chivron's office as its owner - but not occupant - followed with his chaperone.

Downstairs, the three heard noises in the office.

'That'll be Deborah,' Chivron said. He fidgeted in Townsend's grasp. 'Deborah! We're out here!'

'Mr Chivron, is that-' she called from the other room.

'Fool!' Peterson hissed. He nodded to the door. 'Outside. Now.'

Townsend pushed Chivron toward the open door. The door to the office clicked open.

'You said "we", Mr Chivron, what did you...' she said, trailing off.

'Mr Chivron's coming with us.'

'Okay,' she said, holding onto the door frame with skittish fingers.

'Go put the tea on, or whatever it is you do, exactly,' Peterson said. He turned to Townsend. 'Move, now.'

A whistling howl wrapped itself around Norris' form as he lay in bed. It tugged at his slumber, finally coaxing him from his rest. He kept his eyes scrunched up, to keep the real world out. He was tired.

'Not now,' he murmured with a croak. The whistling howl stopped, the thread of cold air ceasing its dance around his body.

He coughed. Then again. The lack of breeze turned into a lack of air. He heaved. Then he opened his eyes. 'Where am I?' It was total darkness, like he'd never removed the blanket. Norris reached out, pushing against the total darkness. It was cold. Cool. Dewey. 'Where am I? Let me out!'

He blinked, suddenly feeling warm. He smelled burning. The woody scent was familiar, almost rural... but above it was the stench of something rotten. Something gruesome was being burned with the wood. With a hand he rubbed his eyes.

The inside of the hut was ominously familiar. Norris' vision returned into clarity from a sleepy blur.

'What do you want? What was that?'

'My resting place,' Bran the warlord said from his chair. 'You have one more chance, Stephen Norris.'

'What do you mean?'

'The evil ones seek to obliterate the resting place within the next turn around the sun.'

'You mean... tomorrow? I don't know what I'm going to do.' Bran indicated to Drest. Norris sighed as the warrior dragged him to his feet. 'Please, I've tried.'

They went outside. The rolling hills were shrouded by purple fog. In the distance, fires burned on the hillsides.

'We burn our dead so their spirits live with the gods.'

That explained the smell of burning flesh. 'Has there been a battle?'

It was evening. Around the rest of the encampment torches flittered in the air.

Bran stopped. 'There are always battles. Use your power, Stephen Norris,' Bran said.

'Power?'

'The gods have imbued you with ability to stop anything. All you need to do is feel the need enough, then you can channel that energy. Haven't you tried it?'

Norris took a gasp, as if to say *no, what on earth are you on about?* But the words didn't come out. He took the gasp, then held his eyes closed.

That gate at the site hadn't moved on its own. He glanced down. His hands were shimmering a golden-yellow, just beneath the skin. He shook his arms and the glimmer disappeared between blinks.

He had, Norris realised. Something had given him that ability to escape with his friend from people who had dishonour running black through their veins. 'I think you're onto something.'

'The power is yours until you expend it, Stephen Norris. The gods believe in you. So do I. Use your power where it matters, or not at all.' Norris avoided Bran's gaze, but the warlord reached out with a dirty hand around his chin. Bran turned Norris to face him. The young man gave a dry, harsh swallow. Bran smiled. 'I do, too.'

'Thanks,' Norris said. 'Tomorrow?'

'The day has come when night turns to light once more. Here and in your future, we will know what will become of our legacy.'

'I'll do what I can,' Norris said through a grimace of determination. 'I won't waste it.'

Deborah looked severely at Norris as he strode through the door to the office that morning. He clocked her gaze and asked three questions: 'Where are they? What's happened? Is Mr Chivron here?'

'No, and don't bother taking that off,' Deborah said, showing with a finger to Norris' coat. 'We've gotta go. You and I. Sorry,' she said to the others. They shrugged. She wound round the desk and pushed Norris out of the door. 'Now.'

'Where are we going?'

'The site. That Peterson and some other man was here when I got here. I think he's finally put the screws on the old man.'

'Shit,' Norris said. 'The bus'll take forever.'

Deborah dug around in her bag and threw a bunch of keys at Norris, who caught them. 'We're not taking the bus. You're driving that.'

'What's that?'

Deborah indicated to a black Mini parked outside the office. She hurried round to the passenger side, waving at Norris to unlock the driver door and get in. He did so and let her in by leaning over and pulling on the door handle.

'Sweet ride,' he said.

'Yeah, it's dad's. He doesn't want me getting buses anymore. You think you know why?'

'Let's not, shall we,' he said, and started the engine. He revved it playfully and like a go-kart the Mini swished into the road and away from the office.

The site soon approached, and Norris parked the Mini along a street of dead houses. Unlike when he was here with Adam on his clandestine trip to photograph the ruins, the streets were packed. Odd, considering the houses were all condemned slums, their broken windows boarded up. Norris got out, followed by Deborah.

'Sounds like a funfair,' she said, homing in on the hubbub of conversation coming from behind the hoardings opposite. 'Is this the site?'

'It is,' Norris said, striding through toward the open gate in the hoarding. 'What are all these people doing here?'

Once he rounded the corner and entered the building site, he found out: dozens of contractors and builders in scruffy, dirty clothing were milling about. Behind him, a truck came to a clattering stop. It disgorged another four people who made for the gate, ignoring Norris. 'That's a council truck!' Norris said, observing the painted logo on the side of the lorry. 'These are all council men. Christ. Like a bloody circus, this.'

'Look, there he is,' Deborah said. 'Peterson.'

'And that's Townsend.'

Norris led Deborah into the site. 'Careful, I don't you tripping up.'

'Least of my worries. Quick, look, he's got Mr Chivron with him.

Norris pushed to the back of the crowd, ducking behind some of the men. Just beyond, on the other side of the pit, Peters was watching a couple of men fiddle with a wooden box that was placed directly in front of him on the lip of the pit. Another man was climbing the ladder, nodding at Peters, who hurried him out with a furtive gesture.

And next to him, observing with a severe look that really said *I don't want to be here, can this all be over* was a pensive and cloying Mr Chivron.

'He doesn't look happy,' Norris said, pushing past a couple of the builders to the front of the crowd. He glanced down. Wires led from the wooden box into the pit. The wires led around the pit toward the excavation that Norris had tumbled down.

'Gents, please,' Peterson called, grabbing everyone's attention. 'Now we get to the main event. As you know, we've had some problems. It's put us behind. But we're here to deliver the solution to those problems, as graciously agreed by Mr Chivron, here,' he waved. 'The best minds in the business have really pulled out all the stops to make this project one we'll be proud of for years to come. So, let's move onto phase two of this grand plan to turn this derelict area of our fair town and the city as a whole into a beacon of modernity.'

'Mr Chivron, would you like to do the honours?' Peterson asked.

'You know what I think,' Chivron said. 'No.'

'What was that? You'll have to speak up in front of all these people whose livelihoods depend on your decision. You don't want them to go hungry and on the dole, now, do you?'

Chivron gave Peters the most withering of stares. 'I suppose I don't.'

'This way,' Peters gestured, guiding Chivron toward the wooden cabinet. A brass handle emerged from the top of it.

'Why are you making me do this?' Chivron growled. 'This is needless theatre.'

'Theatre's never needless, just illustrates my point. You doubted us, and now you can get us back on track. For everyone's sake.'

Chivron groaned and thrust his hand down onto the detonator, forcing it to the base of the cabinet.

Nothing happened.

'It's a dud!' Norris said to Deborah. She smiled, just weakly.

'Don't be so sure,' she said. 'Look, it's him.'

From the shack, the dirty figure of Whelan approached, stomping across the windswept site. He fiddled with the detonator, checking the wiring.

'Seems good,' he said.

'Get down there and find out the problem,' Peters said. Whelan hopped down the ladder. 'You too,' Peterson said to Chivron. 'Go with him.'

'Are you mad?'

'I'll come too, then, if you're going to be such a baby.'

Peterson led Chivron to the ladder. They climbed down.

'Why are they climbing into the hole?' Deborah asked.

'Something's wrong,' Norris said. 'None of this is right at all. You saw those explosives, they could go off at any second. Come on,' he said, dashing past the crowd. He skidded to the top of the foundation pit. 'Sir! Sir!' he called.

Chivron turned. 'Norris, what are you doing?'

'Pipsqueak!' Peterson said. 'Get out of here, this doesn't concern you.'

'What's he doing?' Norris shouted. They turned to see Whelan knelt at one of the packages of explosives with a lighter.

'Are you mad?' Chivron said. 'You'll kill all of us!'

'Wrong type of wire, you see,' Whelan said. He clicked the lighter and the wire hissed. 'Not electric, you see.'

'What do you mean?' Peterson asked.

'Needed a literal light.'

'And you've lit it.'

'Yes,' Whelan nodded.

'We're still in the pit, you maniac! Sod this,' Peterson said, scrambling for the ladder. He thrust his way up it, pushing Norris away. 'Out of the way pipsqueak. I'm not being blown up!'

Whelan turned. 'You're perfectly safe, the fuse is a three minute... oh, hello,' he said, licking his lips at the sight that greeted him at the top of the ladder. 'Pretty little thing for me!'

'Christ no,' Deborah said. 'Mr Chivron, get out of there.'

'I'm coming,' he said, gasping as he reached for the ladder. A couple of rungs up, he stopped. 'Whelan, don't be a madman, you can't stop it now!' Whelan was still fiddling around the packages. He didn't make any moves to move away. 'Get out of there!'

Whelan eventually moved, pushing toward the ladder. He

slipped up it and brushed himself off. 'Hello, pretty,' he said to Deborah.

'Enough, calling me pretty, you creep!' she shouted, slapping him across the face. Whelan teetered, and fell backward, tumbling into the pit again. He grasped with both hands, trying to find purchase on something to stop him falling.

The only thing he grasped was Mr Chivron's coat, and he tumbled too. Then, ground rumbled as a massive roar came from the foundation, and a huge cloud of dust erupted, pockmarked by orange and yellow flame. With a rattle of chips of dirt and loose stone raining down, Norris screamed.

'Sir! Mr Chivron!'

'Get back, boy,' Peterson yelled. 'The old man's had it.'

'Shut up! Shut up, alright,' Norris yelled back at Peterson. He pushed Peterson, his arms shaking. Peterson was thrust back twenty feet in a cloud of rubble and stone chips.

'The hell was that?' Peterson growled.

'Leave him,' Townsend said, helping Peterson to his feet. 'He's jumped into the pit.'

Norris had. It was no longer a pit but a massive, irregular crater. Emerging from the smoke was the shape of a figure on the ground. 'Mr Chivron!'

The form moved a tiny amount, then keeled over. Norris helped Chivron back to his feet.

'I can't feel my legs,' Chivron coughed. He looked behind him. The crypt had been obliterated. 'Wow, that was big. What's that?'

'Come on, let's get you out of here,' Norris said. 'Anyone got a rope? Or a ladder?'

'Wait, just a second,' Chivron said, pausing to turn. He winced in pain, feeling his leg. His hand emerged from its position covered in blood. 'Look what we've done,' he wheezed, looking to where the crypt had once been.

'Christ, ol' Whelan got a faceful,' Peterson said, jumping down. He moved past Norris and Chivron and toward another dark shape on the rough ground. He picked it up. It was an arm.

Chivron shivered and waited to be helped out of the crater. 'This is on you, Peterson, all of it. Now call a bloody ambulance, the fire brigade, the police, all of them! Now!'

Norris felt the wind on his face, though he was fast asleep. It batted on his eyelids, willing him out of his slumber.

He opened his eyes, then closed them as quickly as he had before. Then he opened them.

'Not again,' he thought, seeing the rolling hills of a past time all around.

He turned, expecting to see Bran's hut, but all he saw was burned ruins.

'What's happened?'

'You failed,' a voice called. A hand on his shoulder shook Norris. He was spun around. He saw the elder in all his finery, except this time it was torn and unkempt. Even for a Celtic lord from god knows when, he looked rough. 'You did this.'

'I didn't!' Norris protested. 'I tried, I really did. We all did.'

'No matter,' Bran mumbled. 'Things will take their own course.'

'Why'd you bring me here again, then?! I did my best, surely you can see that.'

Bran sighed. 'Yes, but the gods themselves may be vengeful.'

'So you're not punishing me? There's too much happening, we've got the opening night in a week-'

Bran held up a dismissive hand. 'These things, they mean nothing to me.'

'They do to me!'

'Ask what they mean to the gods, young Stephen Norris,' Bran said.

Then Norris woke, his bed now ruined with sweat as well as the dirt and grime of a thousand years ago.

Norris climbed out of his repaired Marina. Deborah got out

from the passenger side, a flowing pastel pink dress flowing in the breeze. Norris smiled.

'Hardly practical, wasn't it?'

'You said there was a party tonight!'

'I'd have taken you home to get changed,' he said. Then he smiled. 'You look lovely.'

'I like to put in some effort!'

They glanced up. Twenty-three storeys of gleaming, pearl-white concrete and steel shone in the summer sun. Around them, an immaculate swathe of paved area. A few cars were parked here and there, with other wagons nearer to the lobby doors. Men were unloading one of the wagons nearby.

'Come on,' Norris said. They'll be waiting.'

Deborah followed Norris into the lobby. It was light and airy, summer sun streaming through the tall panes of glass, making the lino floor glow. He reached for one of the call buttons for the three lifts. A neon indicator glowed with a click. Above, mechanism whirred and the telltale above the centre door moved down.

'You've met Wilma, right?' Norris asked.

'No, you saw a lot of her when Mr Chivron was in hospital.'

'Don't know how she managed it, with all that.'

'I thought it was a miracle he's walking again. After seeing what happened with that other guy...'

'Yeah, well, he did deserve it.'

'Steve!'

'Did you a favour, blowing himself up.' Norris swallowed. He was remembering that bad dream he'd had the night before, then suppressed that memory. *Not today.*

The lift shuddered and the doors opened. Norris pressed the button for Floor Twenty-Three.

'Was it twenty-three or twenty-four floors, Steve?'

'Twenty-three, then a private staircase to the penthouse. Where Mr Chivron is staying.' The doors whooshed closed, but the lift didn't move. Norris fidgeted, then gave the control panel a slight thump with his palm. Then the doors closed, and the lift took off. 'Still some little issues, you understand.'

'Is that right?' Deborah said, ending with a giggle.

'Come here, you,' Norris said, squeezing the young lady and leaning in for a kiss.

'Stop,' she said, playfully holding back, with no real effort. The lift then shuddered to a rough stop, which ended with a *ping*. The doors then opened with a metallic yawn.

Norris let Deborah leave first, and then followed. 'Up here,' he said, leading Deborah around the back of the lift to a door hidden behind the shaft. 'Private staircase. Up we go,' he said.

They emerged into a small landing, the main wall of which was a curtain of frosted glass, with a door built into the middle. Beyond that, voices and activity. The door opened and a gruff removal man grunted past Norris and Deborah. Seizing the opportunity, the young couple entered, letting the door close behind them.

'Hello?' Norris called.

'Just a moment,' a voice called. 'Wilma, go and say hello, it's Norris.'

A woman entered the open space beyond the door. 'Hi, Stephen,' the woman said warmly. Then her eyes turned to Deborah. 'Hello.'

'Deborah, this is Wilma Chivron. You're looking well. How are you finding the place? You've brought a lot of things,' Norris said. The space was filled with a litany of boxes and packages in rough piles. Wilma gave a grimace. 'Something wrong?'

'Don't let her start,' another voice said, emerging into the space. Mr Chivron entered, wincing and heaving as he walked on his stick.

'Sweetness, stop this movement,' Wilma cooed, but Mr Chivron waved her off.

'Be off, woman,' he said. Wilma shrugged and moved away.

'Penthouse looks nice, doesn't it? All in all, I think we've pulled it together.'

'I'm surprised,' Deborah said. 'After all that with Peterson...'

'Who?' Chivron said. 'Wonder what happened to him,' he said. Peterson had disappeared after the accident that had impaired Chivron and blown Whelan to smithereens. The Tower had taken shape under an anonymous contractor from the depths of the Borough but under Chivron's express direction.

He'd tried to retrospectively right the wrongs of that day by building a strong Tower.

Wilma waddled back in. 'Bloody thing's driving me nuts,' she said, holding her back.

'And you tell me not to exert myself,' Chivron said. From the back room the gurgling of a baby emanated.

'How's Hector?' Norris asked.

'You didn't tell me there was a baby,' Deborah said. 'Oh, how old is he?'

'Eight months. But sweetness,' Wilma said, turning to Chivron, 'He can't sleep in that room tonight.'

'What do you mean?'

'Too much not right.'

'Not right?'

'Let me show you,' Wilma said for the benefit of Norris and Deborah. 'Loose panelling,' she said, pushing on the slats of wood that clad the walls of the living space. 'Loose sockets,' she then said, pushing against the plastic socket outlet with her foot. 'Carpet's wonky, look, you'll see,' she pointed, 'and finally, just in this room alone, the carpet's stained. There's a leak.'

'What's wrong with the boy's room?' Chivron asked. 'These are all... little things.'

'It's freezing, the wind's really rattling the whole wall.'

'Just a little fit and-'

'Enough. I think we should wait until all this is fixed before we spend a night in here. Our old house was *better*.'

Norris grimaced, watching Chivron's eyes bulge at that last word.

Chivron hummed. 'We'll talk about this later. You're coming tonight, I gather,' he said to Norris and Deborah. 'I see you dressed nice and early, Deborah.'

'Of course,' Norris said, referring to the opening party that was planned in the expansive public room on the lobby floor. It was going to be a press launch for the tower with the first residents to move in, after being offered a flat by the council.

'Can I see him, then?'

'Who?' Wilma said. 'Oh, Hector. Come on then, he's very friendly.'

Deborah disappeared with Wilma, leaving Norris and Chivron alone.

'I hope it all goes to plan tonight, Norris, I really do. We might just rescue our reputation.'

'Your reputation?'

'Yes, mine. And yours.'

'Oh, Steve, this is going to be a wonderful evening,' Deborah sighed as she climbed out of the Mini. A light-pink gown clad her svelte frame, and some crystals glistened with the reflection of the light. 'Thanks for driving me.'

Norris smiled. 'Couldn't have a pretty picture like you driving.' They held hands. 'Wonder how Mr Chivron got on?'

'Hopefully alright,' she said. She glanced up at the Tower. So did Norris. The Penthouse wasn't visible from this extreme angle; just the studded concrete of the sides of the Tower.

'I think we did alright, you know,' he said, letting others wander in. He propped himself up on the car bonnet. 'Come here.'

'Steve, we're going to be late!' she said, laughing just a bit. But she turned around and went to him. He put both hands on her hips and pulled her in for a kiss.

'You're very special to me, Deborah,' he said.

'Steve!' she giggled. 'People are here.'

'I don't care about them,' he squeezed. 'I care about you.'

The couple embraced; their faces intertwined.

'Excuse me,' a voice said, breaking the spell. Norris coughed. Then he glanced past Deborah. Who he saw made him smile.

'Adam!' he said. 'Good to see you!' He shook his friend's hand.

'It's been too long, Steve, but I couldn't say no to a party. Everyone's going to be here, all the bigwigs. Look, there's Mr Scaliterri,' he said, waving. A man in a trilby hat waved past and approached.

'Any news on, well, you know who?'

'Nobody's seen him since that day,' Adam said. 'Maybe he has just vanished.'

Norris hummed. 'He's a bad penny. He'll probably show up. Mr Scaliterri,' he said, his cadence becoming warmer. 'Lovely weather isn't it!'

'It's been so all week, Mr Norris. I wasn't sure if I should attend given...'

'Ah not to worry, sir,' Adam said to his superior. 'Steve did his best. We all did.'

Scaliterri murmured pensively. 'I only hope this is true. I'll see you three inside, yes?'

'Sure, Mr Scaliterri,' Adam said. The older man made for the entrance. 'Come on, it's nearly eight-thirty. The invitation said the ceremony to open the tower starts then.'

'Alright,' Norris said. He looked to Deborah. 'Ready to go.'

'I hope I wasn't interrupting,' Adam said. 'You two look great together.'

Norris regarded Deborah and gave a breathy laugh. 'Adam, we'll see where the evening takes us, shall we?'

Inside the lobby, a signpost directed people to the Public Space. The rest of the lobby was lit only by the dying vestiges of the sunshine, which gave the lobby a cool, twilight hue. Norris stopped, seeing a crack of light coming from the wall opposite.

'Wait here,' Norris said.

'What's up?'

'That door shouldn't be open.'

'What's in there?'

'Mechanical. Look,' Norris said to Adam. 'Take Deborah in to get her a drink. I... I just want to be sure.'

Deborah held onto Norris' arm. 'Be careful, Steve.'

'I'm sure it's nothing,' he said. 'Save a glass of champers for me!'

'Alright,' she said, smiling. Adam led her through the doors into the golden glow that filled the public space.

Norris watched her disappear into the waiting crowd and made quickly through the space to the open door. It squealed open.

'What're you doing?' Norris asked the man in overalls that was examining the open power cabinet. A toolbox stood by his feet, with screwdrivers and lengths of wire jutting from it at odd angles.

The man turned his head. 'What does it look like?'

'Surely you should be done by now. What are you doing?' Norris stepped forward.

'Stop there,' the electrician said. 'Who are you anyway? You're one of those fancy party guests aren't you?'

'Yes, but-'

'But nothing, bub,' the electrician hissed. 'It's because of you lot that I'm still working in this bloody place. Be off with you.'

'Alright,' Norris said, turning back. He pulled the door closed behind him.

As he left, a man approached the electrician from behind the door. 'Get on with it.'

'You know what'll happen?' the electrician protested.

'Just do it and be quiet,' the man said, his voice raspy, almost gravelly, thrusting some crumpled notes into the electrician's hand. 'Be ready on my word.'

The lobby was filling with the sounds of music and chatter. He entered through the double doors into the public space. It was filled with dozens of people. Gantries of disco lights hung from the artex ceiling, and on the far side of the space was a stage a couple of feet high.

Norris quickly found Adam and Deborah by a temporary bar in the corner of the room.

'Christ, it's hot here,' Norris said.

'Yeah, kitchen's there,' Adam nodded his head to a door behind.

'Wow, they've packed a lot in here,' Norris said, ducking under one of the light stands. It was only a couple of feet above his head.

Adam shoved a fluted glass in his hand. 'Nearly go-time,' he said. 'What did you see in that maintenance room,' he asked.

'An arsehole electrician,' Norris said. 'They've got a lot of lights in here,'

'It's like a full-on disco,' Deborah said. 'Let's dance later, Steve!' Then she looked beyond the crowd. 'Has she brought the little baby with her?'

Norris took an uncomfortable breath in. Looking past the crowd, he saw Wilma Chivron by her husband's side. The little baby, Hector, was cradled in her arms. Norris shook his head, Deborah already going over there. His attention was turned to the ceiling again. There were a lot of lights, and cables and gantries were pinned to the ceiling. A room envisaged as a bingo hall or quiet space for residents to relax had been turned into a packed, steaming hot discotheque. The beads of sweat quickly permeated Norris' tuxedo and rolled down his brow.

'Have another drink,' Adam said. 'They're on the house.'

Norris smiled and pushed through the clammy crowd toward the bar. He picked up a tall glass of beer. The champagne had tasted sour; he'd only finished it out of good manners.

Then the music stopped with a few clipped taps on a microphone. The crowd whooshed into silence.

'Bugger me,' Adam said. 'It's the Mayor!'

'Ladies, gentlemen, esteemed guests and new homeowners,' a man in a suit called, climbing onto the stage. Ceremonial chains adorned his shoulders. 'Welcome one and all to you for joining this incredible opening of the brand new Chivron Tower. New homes to brighten our horizons,' the man carried on. Norris turned. He felt especially hot now. Behind him, the kitchen door had been opened. Three chefs stood in there turning out canapes out of a couple of small, gas ovens. Waving, Norris turned away.

'And now,' the man on stage said theatrically, 'the guest of honour who'll be living with us all, right on the top floor of his marvellous creation, Mr and Mrs Herve Chivron!'

Everyone's eyes turned to the lobby door. Nobody was there.

'I said, Mr And Mrs Chivron!' the Mayor repeated. 'Fashionably late!'

The crowed gave a pregnant pause then erupted in cheers. Mr Chivron came forward with Wilma, who was cradling little Hector.

Applause radiated through the crowd, which parted to let the architect through to the back of the room toward the stage.

Chivron climbed up and took the microphone. 'Hello?' he said, the mic squealing with feedback. 'Oh, sorry. Well, yes, thank you everyone for this,' he gestured, stammering for words. 'It's so lovely, despite all the pitfalls we had getting here it's... are we all happy with what we've found?' The crowd cheered warmly. 'Thank you.'

The Mayor nodded to a figure who'd emerged from the back of the room. Reaching for the microphone, he took it from Chivron, who was a bit surprised as the words had begun to flow.

'May I add a special visitor who's just arrived,' the Mayor called, 'to see this marvel with their own eyes, it's James Ballard, of the J. G Ballard consortium. They brought the vision to life.'

'Oh, no,' Norris said.

'What?' Adam asked.

'Look at Mr Chivron,' Norris nodded. Adam did so, as did Deborah. His face had fallen wide with despair, then fury. 'Nobody talks about Ballard to him, how could they have done this?'

The crowd parted again and Ballard emerged, a rotund, balding man in a light jacket walking up to the stage. He shook Chivron's hand. The announcer passed the microphone over.

'Give me that,' Chivron growled, but Ballard took the mic from the Mayor, avoiding Chivron's grasp.

'I have to say,' Ballard started, enunciating with a plummy cadence, 'that I am surprised. Pleasantly. Herve,' he said, looking to Chivron with a saccharine smile plastered across his face, 'You may have finally done yourself proud. To a degree.'

'Don't say it,' Chivron said.

'It was Chivron's vision that brought the Tower onto paper,' Ballard started, 'but the work of my firm to really bring that vision to life.'

'Yeah,' Chivron growled, 'and a grand job your cowboys did bringing it to life.'

'Sorry, that was that?' Ballard asked. 'Oh, yes, of course. You were going to thank me for bringing this from your brain to reality. You really know, from all our encounters, you just needed that push, Herve, to really succeed. I was only too glad to be the one to push you.'

'Steady,' the Mayor faltered, his eyes on Chivron.

Beads of sweat appeared on Chivron's forehead. Chivron took a deep breath. His shoulders raised and then he shoved Ballard, nearly knocking him over. The crowd reacted in a wave of *oohs*.

'Oh shit,' Norris said. The crowd murmured, confused, not sure whether to laugh or cry.

'A little accident there, but never mind,' the Mayor said. 'Are you fellows alright?'

Chivron scowled. Ballard did too, dusting himself off. 'As well as can be expected.'

The Mayor scanned the room. The crowd was silent, waiting for whatever was to come next. He cleared his throat. 'Three cheers, I think! For all those that brought the Chivron Tower to life!'

Hip hip! Hooray... the Mayor started. The crowd didn't seem enthused. The Mayor waved. He had seconds to get them back. His eyes flittered to Chivron, then back to the crowd in front of him. *How dare that bastard show me up.*

Hip hip! Hooray!

The crowd was recovering. The Mayor grinned, pulling his hands up for the final cheer.

Hip hip-

'Something's wrong,' Norris said. 'Get out!'

'What? What do you mean?' Adam said.

'Can't you smell it?' Norris said. 'Gas!'

He grasped her hand and pulled, but she didn't move. 'You're scaring me, Steve.'

The crowd cheered as the final *hooray* beckoned, but then the scent wafted into the main room. Then a *fzzt* of current as the lights went up.

It was too late. A fireball erupted from the kitchen, dancing across the ceiling toward the stage.

'Down! Everyone down!' Norris called, falling to the floor as the flames careened across the ceiling above him. This was followed a second later by a larger, throatier fireball that exploded from the kitchen and erupted like a grenade across the public space. People scattered, falling to the floor. In a shower of sparks, three of the lighting gantry tumbled, crushing people under them.

'Mr Chivron!' Norris called. 'Sir, get out of there!'

He glanced to the stage, his view framed by a corona of flames and sparks. The tinsel and synthetic material that decorated the walls and ceilings had ignited and was burning red hot in spits of flames and fire. Smoke billowed from these furnishings, filling the space. In a few seconds, the shocked figure of Mr Chivron disappeared behind a curtain of smoke and soot.

Norris felt a pull on his trouser leg. The sound of the party as now replaced with screaming and howling. He looked down. It was Adam.

'Steve, we've gotta get out, before... oh god,' Adam said, 'the crowd's stuck!'

Norris pivoted, seeing the crowd pile against the only door to the lobby. Dozens of people pushed against the door, creating a logjam. The fire ripped across the ceiling above them, pulling the oxygen of their screams into the flames that consumed the synthetic decorations. Fronds of burning tinsel and decoration rained down on them.

'Steve!' a voice called. 'Steve, help!' It was Deborah.

'I'm here,' Norris called, wading through the smoke. The floor was treacherous, the surface undulating and uneven. It seemed to shift with every step. Norris glanced down and realised he was treading on human forms. He came to a pile of metal equipment where most of the lighting for the stage had fallen. Legs and limbs were splayed underneath, against the floor. A couple of them moved, just enough, propelled by the last vestiges of life. Norris knelt down. The heat was searing from behind. The perspiration on Norris' back felt like it was boiling.

'Wilma!' Chivron called. 'Oh my god... and Hector!'

'Deborah, we'll try to get you out.' Norris looked down. 'She's trapped under the gantry!' he yelled. Chivron moved on the other side and heaved against the wreckage. It moved but only a few centimetres. It was a pointless effort. At the other end, flaming wreckage smouldered. Pockets of fire seemed to be slowly encroaching from the back of the room, from where the kitchen had been. Above, a length of rope draped down from the ceiling to the gantry. Norris reached for it but couldn't reach it.

'Mr Chivron, you may have to try to pull!' he called.

Chivron moved and grasped for the rope. He tugged. The fallen gantry seemed to move with an ugly squeal of metal.

'Bit more,' Norris urged. The older man on the other side heaved, grunting with effort. Norris pushed against the first gantry, pivoting it away. 'Now drop!'

Chivron let go of the rope and the gantry clanged to the ground. 'One more, boy!' he called. Then he sank to his knees and held Wilma's hand. She was prone, pinned to the floor.

'I don't feel so good,' she moaned.

'Shh, shh, it's alright. Where's Hector?'

A wail came from beside Wilma. Chivron fidgeted and reached into the tight spot. He felt a little hand. It was warm. And dry. Both of those things were good.

'Stop right there,' a raspy voice that they'd all almost forgotten said, right from behind. Norris quivered with his friend, glancing over his shoulder.

'Peterson!' he hissed. 'What the hell are you doing here? We thought you were gone!'

'Ha! You'd like that, wouldn't you, pipsqueak.' A sharp metallic click came from Peterson who emerged from the smoke. His face was pallid and grey. 'I see the Mayor couldn't cut it. Shame,' he said, looking to the fallen man in the sash that was surrounded by ashen debris. The chain around his neck formed a noose which glimmered with the flicker of fire.

'We haven't got time for this, help us with the bloody thing so we can get these people-'

'I said no heroics,' Peterson said, pushing the cool metal of the pistol he held into Adam's ribs. He moved it to Norris, jabbing him with the stumpy weapon. 'Nobody leaves.'

The girder dropped. Wilma and Deborah wailed in pain.

'Wilma!' Chivron cried. 'I'm here.'

'Yes, all one big happy family,' Peterson said. 'Live together, die together.' Peterson laughed, but he didn't see the movement in the smoke behind him.

'The hell is that?' Adam asked.

'No talking!' Peterson shouted, waving the gun at the young man. 'You cast me out, after what happened.'

'That was your own fault, Peterson. You wouldn't listen, would you? And look, you've bloody killed the Mayor! I imagined people dying of old age here in years and years, not splatted on the bloody floor! You said it was me, but it was you! You ruined all this!'

'Sir, I can't hold it!' Norris heaved.

'He cast me out too. I was a liability.'

'He wasn't bloody wrong, though!' Chivron shouted. 'Now for once in our partnership, do the right bloody thing that I tell you! Help those guys with that damn beam, before it's too late!'

Peterson laughed and didn't move. Behind him, a rattling. Something was scraping along the wooden floor, but the smoke and soot that billowed from the pockets of fire consuming the entire ground floor of the Tower at this point were covering the source of the movement. Flames glimmered on moving metal. Peters turned, hearing the motion over the low roar and crackle of the flames. 'Who's there? Show yourself!' He waved the pistol around. The sounds continued. 'Get out here!' he yelled, firing blindly into the smoke. Then silence.

A metallic tingling came, like a length of chain was being dragged over the rough and ruined floor. It stopped. Then it pounced. Peterson yelled and disappeared into the smoke with a corset of metal around him that glinted for a split second before disappearing with his figure. Distantly, a metal hatch hammered shut.

'That sounded like one of the waste chutes,' Chivron said. 'It can't be.'

'Let's not worry about that,' Norris said. More ceiling tiles around them were collapsing in fronds of fire. He looked to Adam and grasped the girder. His muscles burned. Norris gasped. His eyes narrowed, and he saw a glimmer of golden light. He knew the power was there. 'You ready? On two. One, two...' he said, heaving with effort. The beam lifted and Wilma stretched, starting the scramble out from underneath.

'I can't hold it,' Adam said.

'Come on, nearly there,' Norris said. He roared, pushing the gantry up. Flames licked along it, across Norris' hands. The skin was turning red, but Norris held on, his knuckles white. Flecks of gold light fizzled from beneath his hands.

'The hell is that?!' Adam called.

'Not now, look, get her!'

'I'm stuck!' Wilma called. Norris glanced down, seeing her caught on a twisted part of the girder. 'Herve, get Hector! Get him, forget me!'

'I'm not leaving you!'

'I'm losing it!' Adam said. More rubble rained down on the girder from the ceiling, which was cracking apart. Dust joined the conflagration of soke and soot. 'Get one of them out of here, or they'll both be squashed!'

Chivron shivered. He tried to grab the beam but it was too hot; he screamed, letting go. 'Wilma,' he said.

That was enough, and she crawled out. From both sides, the parents grasped for the small form of Hector, a heap on the floor.

'The ceiling's going,' Norris called as fire erupted from above. It roared, pulling the entire ceiling down and burying the boy under a heap of rubble. Chivron disappeared from view. 'Come on,' he said to Wilma. 'We've got to get you out of here!'

'My baby!' she wailed, welding herself to the spot with grief. 'I can't leave him, he's there!'

'We've gotta get out, this whole place is going to go,' Adam heaved. He pulled on Wilma and she turned and followed. 'Steve, you too! Time to go!'

'No,' Norris said, hearing the scream from the other side of the room. 'We've got to rescue Deborah, wherever she's gone.'

There was no way Norris and Adam could get out through the exit. They crawled through the ruins of the public space, eventually finding themselves in the burned-out kitchen toward the front.

'In here,' Norris gasped. Pulling himself and his friend out of the hazy, smoke filled space beyond. In the gloom, the orange flashes of fire punctuated through the acrid smoke. 'Christ,' he said, 'the whole place has gone up.'

'Yeah,' Adam heaved. 'How're we gonna get out now, Steve?'

'We're not,' he said. He raised a hand to the inevitable. 'We've got to get her out. She's alive, I know it.'

Adam moved. The party room was a ruin. The small little kitchen was proving some respite, but it wouldn't last forever. Wisps of smoke flowed from the larger space in, rushing... *somewhere*. 'Look,' Adam said. He pointed up.

Norris followed the trail of smoke through the gloom and saw the vent in the ceiling. 'Reckon we could get in there?'

'If we don't,' Adam coughed, 'we're done for.'

'Right, help me get that shelf down and we'll get up there,' Norris said. Adam assented and pulled at one of the metal shelving units that lined the wall of the kitchen. Boxes of ingredients fell to the floor but were quickly forgotten about. With a scrape, the two men manoeuvred the shelf underneath the vent. Norris climbed.

'Careful,' Adam coughed as the shelf teetered.

'Almost got it,' Norris replied, pulling at the grate. His knuckles went white around the concentric oblongs of metal. They wobbled but didn't move. 'Ah, sod it!' Norris called, jumping back down.

'Try again,' Adam urged through fits of coughing.

'I need a lever,' Norris said.

Adam looked about and offered Norris a wooden spoon. Norris's face scrunched up. Then Adam looked to the shelf unit itself. It stood on metal legs about a foot tall at the base. He grabbed one and pulled. The leg wobbled. He gasped, the breath turning into a cough as the smoke filled the room. The leg snapped and the shelf tower lurched with a squeal.

'Shit, nearly had us!' Norris said. Adam handed him the metal leg. 'Cheers.'

'Hurry, Steve,' Adam said, holding the shelf as his friend climbed back up. With a clang, the short pole went between the grille and with a heave, it fell to the floor. Norris scampered up, lying prone in the vent. Adam followed, his friend pulling him up.

The metal duct was a couple of feet high and filled with dust and smoke. It was also pitch black.

'Follow the breeze,' Adam said. Norris did so, fidgeting along the conduit. He stopped dead around a corner.

'Shit, nearly went!'

'What's there?' Adam asked, unable to see.

'A way up,' Norris said. 'Let's go.'

Norris turned around and found he was in a vertical space he was able to stand in. Adam joined, and the two were pressed together.

'Don't get any funny ideas,' Norris said with humour, but Adam didn't laugh.

'Up?'

'I guess so,' Norris said. He held out a hand on each side as Adam ducked. They slid on the metal lining of the shaft. Norris reached up. He found a lip. 'Are you kidding me?'

'What?'

'No lining up here, it's bare concrete!'

'Christ.'

Norris swivelled, continuing to feel with his fingers. 'Aha, think I can feel the first-floor vent. You still got that pole?'

Adam fished around. He passed the piece of metal up. 'Yeah. Here.'

'Great,' Norris said, pushing against the vent cover with the bar. 'Almost got it...' The metal of the cover wailed and then fell out, clattering against the lino floor beyond.

Now the pair had to scramble out. Norris went first, holding his breath. The smoke was getting worse. He glanced behind him just before he vaulted, seeing the smoke fill the tiny space. He was sure the orange fronds of fire wouldn't be far behind. Then he pushed up, jumping, taking the ledge and grappling for some purchase. His hands stopped on the lip of the vent facing outward and he pulled. Finally he gasped, his legs jutting out half-suspended. 'Push me, Adam.' Adam did, grasping Norris' feet and pushing. The legs disappeared, replaced with a pair of hands. 'I'll help you up.'

Norris pulled Adam into the landing. The two men dusted themselves off as they got to their feet. Norris went straight to the window. In the evening vista he saw crowds of people outside. But no fire engines. *Had nobody called them?!*

'How do we get down?' Adam said. From above, a booming rattle came.

'We don't. I think we have to go up,' Norris said, making for the stairs.

'Are you mad?'

'Trust me, alright.'

'Show me your hands.'

'Why?' Norris asked.

'You were holding onto that red-hot beam. Your hands should be ruined.'

Norris held his hands out and wiggled his fingers. The skin was intact–charred and dirty, but intact. 'And yet, they're not.'

'There's some weird stuff going on here, Steve. You know about it, don't you?' Norris didn't answer. Adam sighed haughtily. 'We should get out of here.'

'Not without Deborah. We can't leave her to it,' Norris said.

From above, there was a shriek, followed by some rhythmic thuds. Adam looked to Norris. 'Alright. Let's go.'

The pair raced up the stairway as quick as they could. Each

landing window showed the evening drawing in, the pallid cloud of smoke from the fire on the ground floor pooling up, shrouding the city beyond.

Norris stopped on the Eleventh Floor, bending double for lack of breath. Adam followed.

'I can't go on,' Adam heaved.

'Come on, we've got to.' Around the pair of them was a creaking, a low resonant moaning of concrete and steel. It came from the building itself - not inside or outside. Beyond that, the same shrieking that bedevilled Norris downstairs. He took a haughty guff of breath. Then, exhaling, he stormed up the next stairway.

He only got another floor up before he was pulled to the side of the stairwell by Adam.

'Stop,' his friend asked. 'We're being followed.'

What?! Norris' face said, scrunching with incredulity. But then he listened. Below all the other horrific sounds... the *clomp-clomp-clomp* of footsteps. They were getting closer, steadily approaching like heartbeats.

Norris turned, then screamed.

On the stairway above was the burned and blackened figure... of Peterson. His clothes were charred, falling away in the draft.

'Good bloody God,' Adam said. 'He's...'

Uuuuhhhh the figure of Peterson murmured. Slowly it held out its hands, like Frankenstein in the movies would. Norris ducked, Peterson's limbs responding belatedly like they were coursing through invisible treacle.

Adam smiled, but this angered Peterson who lunged forward, closing the gap in a blur. Adam yelped, pinned against the stairwell wall. The rabid figure held him against the wall with one arm while Norris, shrieking, pulled at the other.

A wet sucking sound followed, and Norris felt the arm pull backward. Bone creaked, then cracked with a sick *schnaaap* before he fell back against the stairwell floor.

Opening his eyes, he saw Peterson's arm in his, laid across his front. But Peterson was still against the wall, pinning Adam to it with his right hand. Peterson's left shoulder had collapsed, a viscous near-black liquid seeping out and dripping onto the floor.

It stunk.

Norris vaulted himself to his feet and grabbed Peterson's shoulder, spinning him round. Peterson's head lolled to and fro, then Adam pushed back from his position against the wall like a coiled spring. Peterson fell backwards and the two men ran upward.

They reached the Twenty-Third floor, but outside the smoke from the fire obscured the evening light, and the landing was in near pitch darkness.

A shriek of terror pierced this darkness. 'Stop! Don't touch me!' the voice said, wailing.

'Deborah!' Norris called, bounding around the lift to the private staircase up. 'I'm here!'

'Steve!' she shouted. Then her voice changed. 'No, don't come near me with that!'

Norris bounded up the final flight of stairs and emerged into a maelstrom. The boxes and belongings piled up against the wall as and partitions were scattered across the floor.

By the corner of the room, Deborah was tied to a column. Norris ran over to her.

'Are you okay?' he asked, grasping her hand. She struggled against the rope and laced her fingers into his.

'Better, thank you Steve,'

'Er, Steve,' Adam said. 'Look at that.'

'What?' Norris replied, tearing himself away from Deborah. 'Oh. Is that you?' he said to the mirror on the wall. It showed rolling hills, fronds of grass moving in a heavy breeze under tumultuous, black-lined clouds.

'That has to be a telly-' Adam started, halted by Norris holding his hand up.

'No,' he said, approaching the glass.

'Don't go near it!' Deborah yelled. 'It's doing all sorts!'

But Norris did, holding out a hand. His fingers closed toward the glass, then touching it...

A blast of energy thrust Norris back to the floor with a flash of light. What looked like a bolt of lightning in the projection on the mirror cast out *from* the mirror into the space. The flash illuminated someone else in the room.

Mr Chivron.

He stepped forward into the middle of the room.

'Sir, what are you doing?'

'He was too weak,' Chivron said with a growl. 'Him, don't you see?'

Norris, Adam and Deborah turned their heads. By the entrance, a figure with one arm lolloped into view.

'Peterson,' Norris spat.

'You see, he didn't have the capacity, at the end of the day,' Chivron said, raising a hand to gesticulate. It trembled wildly. 'He couldn't imagine the power that he had unleashed. What he put into the building. The life he gave the Tower.'

'What're you talking about?'

'They were arguing,' Deborah said. 'Something about... gravel?'

'Aggregate!' Chivron shouted in correction. 'He ordered the rubble ground up into concrete. The very concrete poured into moulds to form the Tower.' Then he chuckled.

Norris went wide-eyed, realising what had happened. 'What do you need from me? From us.'

'You're my protege, Stephen,' Chivron mumbled. 'Join with me to harness this awesome power. The power you've already tasted, yes. You liked it, didn't you?'

Norris held out his hands once again. He curled them into a

ball. 'I know.'

'The power they lent you is gone now, but you can have it for eternity,' Chivron said.

'And do what with it?'

'Live forever and a day.'

'Is this what you want your poxy legacy to be? Look at what's happening.'

Chivron laughed, stepping through the double doors to the rooftop. 'My legacy is shattered. My family destroyed. It's not fair! With this power, this monument... I will call it my mausoleum and convert others to the power.'

Norris stepped to the threshold. 'It won't work that way. You know how this ends.'

Chivron turned. 'You disappoint me. Do you not want to share my legacy?'

'No,' Norris said. 'I'd rather live with my legacy.' He looked to Deborah, his eyes glossing with dew. 'You're my future, darling.'

'Steve,' Deborah said. 'What're you doing?'

Adam tackled Norris to the floor as he stood there, still as a statue. A wave of intense blue light erupted from the ruins of the mirror. Norris got to his feet. Adam was already untying Deborah from her captivity.

'Are you mad, Steve?!' Adam yelled into his friend's ear.

'Christ alive,' Norris gasped. The broken frame of the mirror was forming a solid piece again, the glass turning liquid like, with a tumultuous rippling across the surface. With another flash of light, it fused together as one reflective surface again.

Except it wasn't reflecting anything but had become a window to another world. *Another time.*

Norris ducked as a translucent fist emerged from the mirror. It looked ghostly but pummelled the wall which trembled. Norris rolled forward, getting up as the translucent fist rounded on him again. This time, as it came forward, he pushed the limp form of Peterson into it, and it exploded in a firework of aquamarine fizzles.

'Steve, over here!' Adam called. Norris glanced, seeing Adam and Deborah at the threshold of the stairwell to the penthouse. He ran over, the others taking the first step.

But Norris pivoted. Outside, beyond the maelstrom of pulsing, ethereal energy, Chivron peered past him, to a point in the middle of the empty, ruined space.

'You've got to try got it, sir!' Norris called. The energy howled from the mirror, whipping up his hair, his clothes, any loose items like a whirlwind.

Chivron looked up, past the point in the centre of the room and met Norris's gaze. His eyes lit up, just enough. He put a foot forward a couple of millimetres.

Then, from the floor, metal hooks burst and grasped onto Chivron, dragging him down.

A voice from Norris' nightmares boomed all around: *His body is mine, boy, he is my puppet. Now begone or join him, make your decision.*

'Let's go!' Adam said, pulling his friend down the stairs. They emerged a couple of minutes later, panting and exhausted on the burned-out landing. The fire was out, filling the space with lifeless smoke that sought an exit to dissipate outside.

Emerging from the Tower, the three survivors looked at the bewildered firemen and even more bewildered survivors as they crossed into the grass, turning only to hear a heave as the door to Chivron slammed shut.

Finally, Norris looked to Deborah and embraced her. She wept into his shoulder, sniffling as they parted.

THREE MONTHS LATER

'Are you sure you want to go, Mr Norris?' the fire chief said. 'I can't guarantee it's safe.'

Turning from the window to his office in the Civic Building, Norris nodded. A great stain sat in the very middle of this vantage, and it had to be sorted out.

Chivron Tower.

'Let's go.'

It rained all the way there, the precipitation only getting worse, banging on the roof of Norris' repaired Marina every inch of the way. By the time they arrived at the hoarding that surrounded Chivron Tower it was pouring down the glass far faster than the pathetic wipers could dismiss.

Norris got out first, letting the cold autumn rain douse his hair.

'Come on, this won't take long.' The fire chief said, opening the gate to the site. Norris took one glance up at the imposing tower, its facade still stained by smoke and soot from the fire. He paused, taking in a large gasp of chilly air.

The fire chief unlocked the lobby door and Norris went in. The air was damp, the smell of rot and burnt remains lodging themselves right up Norris' nose.

'Structure's still sound, from as much as we've been able to look,' the chief said.

'Oh?' Norris said. The chief nodded to the door. Norris pulled. It wouldn't open, though it shifted, as if on the other side ten tons of glue held it back.

'The concrete's incredibly strong,' the chief continued. 'Nothing we've done can touch it. Chisels, hammers... we tried taking the door off but it's as if it was welded.'

Norris sniffed. *Welded is one word for it.* 'Can you give me a minute?'

The chief shrugged. 'Be my guest. I'll wait in the car. Though

I don't know what you expect to find.'

Norris watched him leave. The moment he did, the door snapped shut. 'What do you want?' he said aloud. Then he held a hand up. 'I see. You let me in for a reason.'

The stairwell door up opened. It snapped open and shut like the jaws of some macabre alligator. 'No, I don't think so. What do you want?'

'Legacy,' a voice called from above. 'Protect the legacy.'

'I'm signing the condemnation order today.' Norris said. He felt another breath of cold, icy wind that made the hairs on his neck prickle. He wanted to say demolition but the chief was right. Nothing seemed to touch this building. It was frozen on the day it opened and had closed, taking twenty-three souls in a space only a stone's throw from where Norris stood. He glanced to the blackened ruin of the public space.

He'd seen enough. And besides, he had his own legacy to consider now. Deborah was expecting, and he'd just made an offer on a nice house in the country. Sussex. A little hamlet called Adversane, just outside Billingshurst. The names of the towns seemed quintessentially anonymous.

It was a bungalow.

ACKNOWLEDGEMENTS

Thank you for reading *Foundations*! I sincerely hope you enjoyed it and that it has whetted your appetite for more of my writing, and that you had as much fun reading this story as I did writing it!

Writing *Foundations* and *Nightmare Tenant* has been an absolute blast and I'm thrilled, excited and so proud of the results of this work, especially as the world goes through a strange and challenging time.

In shaping *Foundations* I can't thank my long-term and trusted critique partner and friend **Chris Kenny** enough for his motivation, inspiration and guidance throughout the writing of *Foundations*. He also read an early draft and it was his suggestions that I feel took *Foundations* over the top to what I feel is a great story.

Thanks to all the members of the **Author Pals Discord server** who offered gracious and fantastic support for *Nightmare Tenant*, without which I wouldn't have been inspired to write *Foundations*.

But the biggest thanks must be extended to you, the reader, for giving up your time to read my story. I hope I have not just met your expectations but exceeded them. Thank you for joining me on my author journey. *Foundations* is only the beginning and I look forward to your company on the road ahead!

ABOUT THE AUTHOR

Richard Holliday is an author from London. He graduated in 2018 with a degree in Creative Writing with English Literature from Kingston University. He has been writing since a young age, initially with an interest in science-fiction, but is also emerging into the horror and thriller genres. He lives with two cats.

Discover more of Richard's work and sign up to his newsletter at
richardholliday.co.uk

WANT TO KNOW WHAT HAPPENS NEXT?

Read *Nightmare Tenant* by Richard Holliday today!

Available on Amazon as a Kindle eBook and paperback!

Where occupancy becomes *possession*!

For years, Chivron Tower was abandoned and left to rot as the world turned. Looming in the skyline a desolate, abhorred ruin; a forgotten relic of the past.

That was how it should have stayed.

But now, the Tower has been resurrected and shown a renewed lease of life, ready for a new generation of families to move in.

Great hope for this restoration is soon to be extinguished. A mysterious tenant is angry, is without mercy and is hungry. It feeds on suffering, making things go bump in the night. It brings more victims to its lair. The warnings it gives turn to torment it revels in.

Joel Barton and his family find they are trapped, with the last remaining residents, good and bad, as they realise escape means confronting a...

NIGHTMARE TENANT

Praise for *Nightmare Tenant*

I finished this book in one sitting, it was such a page turner and I was desperate to find out what happened and the pages kept getting turned and that is a credit to the writing of Richard, who has excelled with creating suspense, tension and genuine horror in this wonderfully crafted novella.I finished this book in one sitting, it was such a page turner and I was desperate to find out what happened and the pages kept getting turned and that is a credit to the writing of Richard, who has excelled with creating suspense, tension and genuine horror in this wonderfully crafted novella.
Chris Kenny, author of *Original Earth Chronicles: The Golden Pyramid*

Richard created an action-packed, spooky tale, a haunted house story but instead of a rambling building, it all takes place in a giant London tower block. He's created a great, fully fleshed-out cast of characters. Richard does a great job of pulling you into the story using the main family in the story, so we really get a feel for their plight, and the adventure pulls you along to a rapid, scary finale! I will never be able to drive past a tower block again without remembering this story.
Victoria Wren, author of *Wild Spirit: The Curse of Win Adler*

Set in an old tower block, I found the visuals and descriptions were perfect in setting the scene in a place that's been quickly tarted up! The author did a great job of having a variety of characters from all walks of life, alongside a sprinkle of humour throughout this thrilling horror story! An excellent read and I can't wait to see more from this author! Though I'm now put off from ever living in a tower block...
Dan Hook, author of *Displaced*

If you're in the market for a High Rise inspired, Dr Who-esque horror tale, this may well be the story for you! Loads of characters, amazing concept and some pretty Final Destination style goings-on, Nightmare Tenant is nothing if not a fun, quirky spin on the haunted house trope you think you know so well.
Hannah R. Palmer, author of *Number 47*

Richard Holliday creates a unique experience with several characters. For such a small book, it packs a punch. I don't want to give too much away but...not everything is as it seems. If you like mysteries, horror, and strange characters, this is for you!
Bethany Votaw, author of *Scribbles and Scrawls*

Nightmare Tenant is an edge of your seat psychological thriller that grabs hold of the reader on page one and doesn't let go until the satisfying conclusion. The story is engaging with the ominous building becoming one of the most menacing characters. A thrill ride from start to finish. I look forward to reading more from Richard Holliday in the future.
Barrett Laurie

Mr Holliday has a way of drawing you in, that to me, was reminiscent of the late, great, James Herbert. In taking the haunted house tale into a hastily refurbished tower block, the author gave a fresh and chilling twist to one of my favourite tropes. This, combined with the author's deft touch for evocative description and believable characters, meant I was invested in the story from the start. I thoroughly enjoyed this novella and would recommend it to anyone who enjoys their horror action-packed, unpredictable and written with style. As I live in a fourteen floored tower block [although a much cleaner, healthier and safer one than the one in this tale] having read this, I'm steering clear of the upper floors once darkness falls.
Colin Clark

Don't miss any of Richard's news and updates - sign up to his monthly newsletter today for new projects, thoughts, recommendations and more! You'll get exclusive access to new pieces of Richard's fiction not available anywhere else!

Sign up at **richardholliday.co.uk**
or scan the QR code on this page:

Printed in Great Britain
by Amazon